Further Jean Rollin books to be announced.

The following videos by the great Rollin
are available on video from Redemption Films.

Requiem for a Vampire
Le Frisson des Vampires
La Vampire Nue
Le Viol de Vampire
The Living Dead Girl
Fascination

Little Orphan Vampires

by Jean Rollin

REDEMPTION
BOOKS

Originally published in France
by Fleuve Noir as Les deux orphelines vampires

First published in the UK by Redemption Books, 1995.
A division of Redemption Films Limited,
BCM PO Box 9235, London WC1N 3XX.

A catalogue record for this book is available from the
British Library.

ISBN 1 899634 25 8

Printed in the UK by
The Guernsey Press Company Limited.
Cover and photographic section printed by
Colin Clapp Printers.

Little Orphan Vampires

Vampires

by Jean Rollin

Beginning with **Le viol du vampire** in 1968, French director *Jean Rollin* has made 15 films. Most of them have been in the horror/fantasy genre. He's often described as a maker of 'sexy vampire' movies. Yet what really makes his films interesting is not the sex, but the unique fairy tale quality that many of them have.

This is the aspect of his work that surfaces most strongly in the books he has written. **Little Orphan Vampires** is the first of *Rollin's* fictions to be available in English and, although it has horrifying sequences, it's the romantic, almost whimsical, quality of the story that will surprise many readers.

Another side of *Rollin's* work that comes out in the present book is his love for the old magazine serials, what the French call *feuilletons*. One of the most popular and successful of these series in France featured the antihero Fantômas. An astonishing 32 of these book-length serials were written between 1911 and 1913 by the journalists Marcel Allain and Pierre Souvestre. **Little Orphan Vampires** includes a direct reference to one of the Fantômas books, **La livrée du crime** (The Uniform of Crime), as well as being itself the first in a series of five books that tell the increasingly bizarre tale of two blind female vampires.✶

Readers who know *Rollin's* films will probably be aware that many of them feature twin female leads. The book he wrote before the present one, which was called **Les demoiselles de l'étrange** (The Sisters of Mystery), also featured two female protagonists who become caught up in a variety of terrifying and mysterious quests involving the Medusa, werewolves and other strange creatures. The book was planned as part of a series, but unfortunately sales were not strong enough to convince the publishers that such an approach was viable. As a sort of revenge, *Rollin* decided to create another female duo who would be in many ways the opposite of the pair from **Les demoiselles**. In that book they had powers of clairvoyance and were almost archetypically 'innocent'. In the present book the girls are both blind and amorally 'evil'.

Rollin sold the idea to Juliet Raabe of the publishers Fleuve Noir. She was looking for a series of horror stories that were to be in a style the French call *romans de gare*. Literally this means 'station novels'—or books to read on the train; what we would call pulp fiction. *Rollin* took as his starting point a famous French melodrama from 1874 called **Les deux orphelines**. This was a typical sentimental weepy, with two starving waifs at the mercy of the evil city of Paris. *Rollin* turned the story on its head, made the girls the aggressors and their victims the innocent benefactors who try to 'save' them. French readers would recognise at once the element of parody. Hopefully some of the black humour of the original survives in this present translation.

Pretty soon it was obvious that **Little Orphan Vampires** had outgrown its pot-boiling origins. Consequently *Rollin* was asked by Christian Garraud of Fleuve Noir to create another series, called Frayeur (Fear). This was an attempt to see if the special flavour of *Rollin's* films could be transferred to the written word. The remaining four episodes in the story of the little orphan vampires have appeared under the Frayeur label, along with other writers' work, chosen by *Rollin* to complement his own particular brand of literary horror.

Pete Tombs, 1995

❝ Clack clack clack clack,' went the white sticks along the linoed corridor. The children who lived on the top floor of the Glycines orphanage watched sadly as the two little blind girls made their way down to the sick bay. They always walked alone like this from room 136 where they lived.

Henriette and Louise didn't sleep in the big dormitories with the other children but in a separate, twin bedded room, just like the staff and the teachers. Because of their special condition they enjoyed certain privileges.

The good doctor Hogineau, who lived in the village near the orphanage, was waiting in the little room that served as both office and surgery. Twice a month he came to visit the inmates. Today he had brought a friend, Dr Dennery, the famous eye specialist from Paris.

'Clack clack clack clack,' went the iron tipped white sticks. The girls' fresh young faces showed no trace of emotion. Calmly, Henriette and Louise stopped in front of the open door, facing the doctors who both stared out at them with the same misty-eyed look.

Dr Dennery turned towards his friend.

"Have they been blind since birth?"

"I don't think so. They say that when they were little they could see. And then something happened that we don't really know much about. They tell us that when they were still children all the colours disappeared."

"The colours? They can't see colours?"

"That's right. They see everything in black and white."

"That's impossible."

Astonished, Dr Dennery turned to the two orphans who were holding each other meekly by the hand, waiting for his question.

"Is it true what Dr Hogineau has just told me? The colours all went?"

"Yes, and then the pictures," Henriette said.

"Now there's only the darkness," Louise explained.

"The pictures have gone for good," Henriette went on.

"Now it's all over and we'll never see again," Louise concluded, pulling a face as though she were about to start crying.

The two men were upset.

"But...have they been examined?" The eye specialist asked.

"Of course. In the town. And even in Paris. Their blindness is inexplicable, but apparently very real."

"Don't you believe us?" interrupted Louise, her voice trembling.

Dennery was touched, he smiled as he stroked the little blind girl's carefully combed hair.

"But of course, my dear. I believe you."

To convince himself he quickly waved his hand, the fingers wide apart, in front of the two pairs of eyes. The girls didn't blink. He pretended to punch them in the face. They didn't flinch. They sensed the movements, however.

"What's happening?"

"What are you doing?"

"You're moving very quickly."

Louise, apparently the more nervous of the two, pressed herself up against Henriette. She put her arm around her shoulder in an instinctive gesture of protection. Fascinated, without taking his eyes off them, Dr Dennery asked: "Are they sisters?"

"No one knows. They are orphans."

"Have they been here a long time?"

This question was put, not to Dr Hogineau, but to sister Martha, the assistant director of the Glycines orphanage, who had just come into the room and was standing with her hands on the girls' shoulders to put them more at ease.

"Seven years. The police brought them when they were very young and since then...they've been as they are now."

"Where are they from? Who do they belong to?"

"From nowhere and to no one. They were foundlings."

Sister Martha wasn't one to mince her words, even in front of the girls.

Dennery raised the two little faces towards him, frowning as he looked at them. Then he led them into the sick room. They were each made to sit down on a chair. They allowed themselves to be led, docile, but not for an instant did they let go of each other's hand.

The doctor examined them in silence. He shone the light of a little electric torch onto their pupils, put some drops into their eyes, did everything that he could to make an assessment. But, finally, he was unable to come up with any diagnosis.

"Do they have any special symptoms?"

"Yes," sister Martha felt obliged to say. "The light seems to hurt their eyes a little. Daylight, I mean. Not electric light."

"Really. The wavelength, maybe?"

"I don't know, doctor. When they're out walking it hurts them if the sun is shining. They can only put up with dull weather and overcast skies. And even then they complain and feel uncomfortable."

"There's probably something important in that. They'll have to be watched much more closely..."

"These are the only blind children in the institution. We can't afford to bring in an eye specialist every week!"

Dr Dennery understood what they were waiting for, and why Dr Hogineau had asked him specially to come to look at the two girls while he was in the neighbourhood. He was believed to be rich, they would certainly know that he was a widower with no children and that he lived alone in a huge mansion in one of the most exclusive parts of Paris.

His curiosity was definitely aroused. And the two girls had moved him without him really knowing why. He said: "If you deal with the administrative formalities, I'll take them back with me. I can easily teach them their way around the house. There is a little garden with a wall around it. I can keep them under permanent observation for as long as it takes. What do you think?"

Sister Martha had tears in her eyes. Henriette and Louise seized the doctor's hands and covered them with kisses.

All this fuss made him uncomfortable and he soon put a stop to it.

"I have to attend a conference in town this evening. Deal with everything, present my case to the board of governors, of course, and arrange as soon as possible my legal guardianship. Meanwhile I shall take them with me to Paris. Get them ready after lunch tomorrow."

He nodded briefly to Dr Hogineau, bowed to sister Martha, kissed Henriette and Louise on the cheek and then strode swiftly away.

Everyone waited until the sound of his steps had faded. Then at last sister Martha and Dr Hogineau allowed each other a look of quiet satisfaction. As for the two girls, they fell into each other's arms, sobbing with emotion.

It was night. All seemed quiet in the Glycines orphanage. No lights were on in the dark and sombre edifice.

Yet a keen observer, with very sharp eyes, would have detected some strange movements in the vicinity of room 136.

Soft whispers filled the air, coming from the two neighbouring beds. It was after 11 o'clock, Henriette and Louise were talking in low voices, hatching some sort of plot.

The excitement of the new life that was due to begin the following morning was keeping them awake.

They both got up and moved to the window. Outside the moonlight shone, it was a sweet, enticing spring night. Without saying another word they pushed open the door that led to the dim, deserted corridor. The words they shared as they left their room, after having slipped pillows between the sheets to give the impression of sleeping bodies, were astonishing words to have come from two blind little orphan girls.

"Have you seen how clear the night is?"

"And how still the countryside is, how peaceful."

"Yes, and that poor little dog going down to the river."

"A lost animal, all alone."

"Let's follow him!"

They tip toed down the staircase to the entrance hall. The feel of the cold flagstones under their naked feet made them shiver, the night air pierced their thin pyjamas... Somewhere a window was open. They were shivering as they reached the huge entrance door which, from long practice, they opened without a squeak. The night air swirled around their bodies. Clenching their frozen backsides, the two girls stepped outside and closed the door behind them. With a few quick bounds they were in open countryside.

They looked at each other, wide eyed, laughing softly to themselves.

It was no longer the cold of the corridor and the hall that they felt, but instead the delicious balminess of the soon-to-be-summer night.

Then they were running along the road, catching up with the

lost dog. They skipped past the cemetery wall. Behind them, the dark, forbidding shape of the Glycines orphanage. Ahead, far off in the distance, the first lights of the village. That noise sounding in the night is the squeak of the cemetery gate. The chain that holds it together is loose, the dog is already through the gap and now they see him scratching up the earth between the gravestones.

Henriette and Louise slip through into the little cemetery in hot pursuit. Laughing, they chase after the dog as it jumps up onto the stones, snapping at them, joining in with their game. Finally, gasping for breath, their cheeks flushed, they stop to look at each other. Excitement fills their faces, just as each one of them fills their eyes with the image of the other. They see. They see each other, and for them it's a mad, deep, heady pleasure: to see and to be seen.

"Look Louise, just beside you, that poor little bat hanging by its claws from that iron cross."

"That's you, Henriette!"

"And you're that snake, Louise, slithering down there through the gravestones."

"Yes, I'm the serpent god."

"The plumed serpent of the Aztecs, and I'm the bat goddess that they worship."

"The bloodthirsty gods are the most beautiful ones."

Suddenly they fall silent and a mysterious light makes their eyes sparkle.

They turn to look at the dog, who sits expectantly on a gravestone, wagging its tail. Henriette waves her hand in front of him to distract his attention while Louise creeps round behind him. Quickly she seizes the animal, who has no idea what these two pretty, happy little girls intend. Louise takes hold of its jaw and pulls its head sharply back, offering up its throat to Henriette, who flings herself forward and sinks her teeth into it. The dog stiffens, twitching a couple of times, but Louise holds it firm. As its life ebbs away Henriette draws back and takes hold of it so that her friend can have her turn. They have to be quick before the creature dies. And so Louise also plunges her teeth in, just above the gaping wound that Henriette has made.

They throw the dog's body away. Taking each other gaily by the hand, Henriette and Louise jump from tomb to tomb, as though they are dancing, their little heads shaking, the hair flapping around their faces. Joy is written all over them, the joy of sight, and of the colours, in spite of the night: the whiteness of the new tombs, the dark green of the wild grass, the pink of their pyjamas, and the red, purple, dark, heavy colour: the blood that smears their smiling mouths.

The village bell sounded midnight.

It was time to go. They left the cemetery and ran, hand in hand, back to the Glycines orphanage. Minutes later they were in their room. With the door firmly closed they lay down in bed together and, hidden under the sheets and covers, began to read forbidden books.

Using a little electric torch stolen from sister Martha, wrapped in the warmth of each other's bodies, they devoured the printed lines, gorging themselves on the corrupting images. They each felt the reassuring warmth of the other's body with a disturbing pleasure that thrilled them. Every evening, wild eyed, they would pour over this book that had become *their* book.

Now they were no longer orphans but Aztec goddesses and the drawings that they looked at, whispering in low voices, showed with disarming frankness the human sacrifices that were performed just for them.

"The blood of this victim, see how it flows."

"And look at this naked man, see how he squirms on the stone."

"Where are we?"

"Here...The serpent god...The bat goddess..."

"Carved onto the altar..."

"Shhh! I can hear sister Martha coming."

They crawled under the covers to hide their girlish giggles.

In the Chestnut Trees Hotel Dr Dennery was getting ready for sleep.

He put out the bedside lamp, his thoughts filled with the tender image of his wards: hardly out of their childhood, with their little plaits, pleated kilts, white socks and patent shoes.

Two pious images from a picture book. The good doctor sensed nothing ambiguous about these two sweet children who got up in the middle of the night to quench their thirst with fresh blood in country graveyards. Cute little girls who, like cats, like hyenas, like tigers, could see in the night.

"Clack clack clack clack," went the two white sticks.

Each holding a cardboard suitcase, Henriette and Louise followed the mother superior and sister Martha down the big staircase, across the hall and out onto the front steps where Dr Dennery was waiting.

It was the day of their departure. The two girls screwed up their faces, dropped their white sticks and covered their eyes with their hands: the sun was out and was burning them. The doctor quickly handed them each a pair of dark glasses, a sort of farewell present. Thus protected, Henriette and Louise tenderly kissed the mother superior and sister Martha farewell and climbed into the car that was to take them to Paris.

Dr Dennery was with them. He had hired a car and driver for the journey, wishing to spare his young protégés the taunts of the rough types who travel on the trains. The car set off and left behind the orphanage of Glycines. They drove past the cemetery. The gravedigger stopped to watch them, abandoning for a moment the hole he was making to bury the dead dog he had found that morning.

Henriette and Louise soon knew from the noise all around them that they had entered a new phase of their life, they were now city girls.

The car crossed Paris by the banks of the Seine and came to a halt near the Rue des Eaux, in front of the doctor's house. In fact it was almost a mansion, with a little garden in front and a door set in the wall.

Dennery spent the rest of that day guiding them around the house. Starting with the ground floor, the big curving staircase and the first floor. Then came the two living rooms, the dining room, the kitchen, the study, his bedroom and finally their very own room, the former guest room, along with some rooms that they didn't really understand-the laundry, a junk room, the library and the games room.

At the same time as he guided their fingers, making them feel the walls, the furniture, the angles and the shapes, he told them what it was that they were touching. They laughed, for them it was a game: getting to know the contours of what would become their new universe. Because it was obvious to this man that the two blind girls would not be going outside. He had it all mapped out for them, a walk in the little garden, between the porch and the entry gate, a few dozen yards more or less. The wall that enclosed the house was their guarantee of safety...for he believed it would take a long time, months, years, to discover, diagnose, care for and, perhaps, cure them.

Henriette and Louise explored the house and the garden with their fingers. But, as night came, they began finally to make out the shapes of things. Sight returned, and with it the marvellous power of looking. They no longer knew what day-time was, they didn't care about the sun and the brightness of the light. But they knew better than anything else the softness of the colours that came with twilight, the subtlety of stones in shadow, the shape of their beds, of tables, furniture, only just visible in the blue tint that surrounded them.

This transition from daily blindness to night-time sight happened softly, progressively. First there was a blurring, with shades of black and white. Then, gradually, the colours. And with them the blue tint that was their daylight.

Later, at dawn, would come a strange moment when the colours of the night were bleached away by a cruel white that marked the onslaught of day. This would be their night until twilight.

Thus passed the first weeks. Their earlier insecurity gave way to a reassuring feeling of confidence. The doctor's guard began to relax. He was sure that the danger period had passed, and that the two blind girls were now quite safe within the confines of his house and garden. He was totally trusting and could not know that the night belonged to them alone. He knew nothing of the savage and cruel life his protégés entered every evening as the shadows lengthened and sight, softly, timidly, overtook them.

They began with brief walks round the garden, then into the street, going further with each trip. Finally the time came when they dared to risk their first night-time adventure. They headed straight for the little cemetery of Passy, through which they wandered like spooks, on account of their full-length night shirts, with lacy collars and cuffs, that Dennery had chosen to replace their orphanage pyjamas. With the wind pressing the cotton against their bodies, or puffing it out like a veil, they looked like two gentle ghosts, twirling about in their winding sheets.

But was anything else, human or animal, likely to come to the cemetery that night?

That was the problem. At first, behind the locked gates, they felt a great sense of release. After so many hours of blindness they revelled in the return of their sight. They read the inscriptions on the gravestones, laughing at some of the convoluted names. They tried to make out the faded but fascinating colours of the garlands of artificial flowers. But soon they tired of these games. The desire to kill had seized them. They were in the right place, now it was time for action. This second part of the night, just after midnight, was reserved for the chase...The pleasure of sight regained had passed. Now they wanted to find a throat to cut, a tender stomach to slit open with their sharp teeth, a plump pair of buttocks for them to sink their fangs into, like hungry young wolves. Just thinking about it made them lick their purple lips with their pink tongues. It was as though they already felt the hot, sticky liquid flowing down inside them....Their eyes, filled before with the simple joys of seeing, now became cruel and alert like those of night-hunting beasts. The little orphan vampires dragged themselves up onto the cemetery wall and looked down over Paris.

It was midnight, and the cities' night life was buzzing. Even here, in the Trocadero, there were adventures to be had. Henriette and Louise could hear footsteps, glimpse huddled silhouettes, detect rendezvous in doorways.

All they had to do was choose.

They climbed back down.

"Look, there's a dog down there."

"Dogs are no fun any more. Don't you remember the last one?"

"In the cemetery near the orphanage."

"I can still taste that horrible clump of fur that I had to spit out!"

"You're right. We're city girls now, not peasants."

"We should at least try for something better."

"Humans, then?"

"Yes. Soft. Young. Full of rich blood."

"It isn't fair. Healthy kids only go out during the day. And we can't see anything then."

"It must be chucking out time for the theatre."

"You're right....Look over there!"

They left the cemetery and, with the white night shirts clinging to their tender bodies, they crossed the square to the steps of the Palais de Chaillot. There was an exit there for one of the theatres. A noisy crowd was just breaking up. Some of them decided to walk through the gardens.

Henriette and Louise crossed quickly over the terrace and made their way into the dark pathways that led down to the Seine.

So did Arthur Dumaine. He was 17 years old and out all alone. His parents hadn't been worried about him going to the theatre. Since they lived in Passy they knew that it took no more than a quarter of an hour to get back home. All the same, his mother had warned him to stay away from the gardens at night, on account of the homosexual meetings that took place there, which, she believed, could have a bad influence on her son's nascent sexuality. In a hurry to get back home, Arthur had decided to ignore her advice. In any case, at this time of night the gardens were deserted-the gay young things were long gone.

Then, as Arthur came up to the roller skating rink just a few steps from the main road, he stopped in his tracks.

A strange apparition was visible in the middle of the rink.

A sort of child-woman, so far as he could see, quite slim and slender, but soft and inviting.

She was naked, and her white body cut through the blackness of the night. Arthur stood there, his mouth agape. Rooted to the spot, he stared at the silhouette which suddenly began to move. At first she began to sway just like a snake, standing in one place, feet together, bending her body back and forth, her long curly hair swaying across her shoulders. Then she began to dance to the sound of a music that, in the silence all around, only she could hear. She leapt, racing from one side of the skating rink to the other, gyrating like a nymph, raising her arms, stretching them out, arching her stomach towards a dumbfounded Arthur, then coming back, leaning over, seizing her plump little behind in both hands, standing in front of him again, stroking her hands, the fingers spread wide, over her budding breasts, over her thighs, over her belly, holding her waist as she bent over.

Arthur stepped forward, pushing his hand into the pocket of his trousers to hold back the erection which the spectacle had inspired.

He was standing then just beside the little kiosk that during the day sold drinks and biscuits to the kids. Suddenly something fierce and heavy, that until then had been hidden on the roof of the building, leapt down onto his back. Arthur fell to the ground as Louise, kneeling on top of him, plunged her teeth between his shoulder and neck, right next to the collarbone where the flesh was thick. Then Henriette came running up to them and, just as excited as Louise, tugged with both her hands at the boy's shirt and jumper, baring his side into which she bit savagely, burying her teeth. Instantly she felt the blood flood into her mouth and she closed her eyes in pleasure as her victim jerked and let out a scream. She bit harder, her teeth clenched as she pulled away, gripping in her mouth a huge lump of tender and juicy flesh that she gobbled down. Then she opened her eyes again and saw her friend gorging herself on Arthur's belly, just below the navel. Louise, seeing Henriette standing up, raised her face for a second to look at her. The blue light, which was their night-time sun, showed her smeared with red, purple drops falling from the corners of her mouth like dreadful tears.

Her face glowed with such happiness, with such love of life and of the world, that it was impossible not to forgive her the murder of this drab young man.

Henriette kneeled down beside Louise. Both of them, breathless, eager for fresh discoveries, looked down at the unconscious Arthur.

Louise murmured: "Have you eaten some?"

"A huge bite."

The wound in Arthur's side gushed blood. The heavy liquid

was soaked up by the earth.

"It's a pity to let it go to waste like that."

"I'm going to paint myself!"

Henriette plunged both her hands into the blood, right inside the wound, and began to smear her naked body with the red liquid.

Soon she was covered from head to foot. Her skin gave off an acrid smell, her eyes shone, glorious in the night, as she breathed in deep draughts of cool air.

Louise, still on her knees beside the body, said huskily: "You look beautiful, all moist with his blood."

In a voice also strangely changed, Henriette replied: "It feels good to be all sticky with this fool's life, watching it flood all over me."

Arthur moaned, twitching faintly.

"We'd better finish him off," said Louise calmly.

"Right," Henriette replied. "But let's make it interesting."

"Do you know what little boys are made of?"

"I think so, but you're right, let's find out!"

Louise opened Arthur's trousers and took out his cock.

Both of them gazed at it in silence, with wide open eyes, which, in the dark night, *saw*.

"And now what?"

"Bite his throat open."

"What about you?"

"It'll be my turn tomorrow."

Henriette, intoxicated by the sight of this thing that Louise held in her hand, threw herself onto Arthur's neck and in a few bites had opened his throat from ear to ear. Louise went on gazing thoughtfully at the cock that she held, while all the time hearing the terrifying sounds of Henriette's frenzy.

Finally it was over, and the two girls left the body there, heading back in the direction of the Rue des Eaux. It was just one o'clock in the morning. Day was not yet due. They had plenty of time.

Henriette was still naked, soaked with blood. She held her night-shirt in her hand, rubbing her thighs as she walked just to feel the dark liquid that was smeared all over them.

Seeing her, Louise pulled off her own night-shirt to be like her friend. In this way the two of them, hand in hand, arrived at the doctor's house. They opened the gate, came into the garden, took a few steps and then suddenly stopped: light was streaming from one of the ground floor windows...

They came closer and saw Dr Dennery sitting at a table in front of the window. He was writing in a big book by the light of a desk lamp. No doubt the results of his latest researches. He need only to have raised his eyes to see his protégés standing naked in the garden at one o'clock in the morning, with Henriette covered in blood and smelling like a slaughterhouse.

Louise turned as though about to run, but Henriette held her back: "Wait...Let's have some fun!"

"Dangerous fun."

"Yes. I bet you I can have a piss under the window without him hearing me."

"All right," said Louise with a shaky voice.

Henriette squatted down. Absorbed in his work, the doctor saw nothing, heard nothing. Henriette stood up, triumphant.

"Did you see?"

"I love you," said Louise ecstatically. "Cover me with your blood!"

Not bothering to wait, she pressed herself against Henriette, rubbing herself against her, so that she too was smeared with their victim's blood. This terrifying sight took place in front of the window, only a few steps away from the good doctor, who didn't once look up. Had he done so, perhaps he would have died from shock at the sight of these two she wolves drunk with bestiality and full of joy, like a pair of children rolling in the mud right under their parents' noses.

Then they looked at each other as though, having stopped misbehaving, they were resuming a conversation that had been started long before. A conversation that had been interrupted by this need to be naughty, this deliberate act of perverse will that was nobodies' business but theirs.

So it was that everything they did remained their secret. Whether it were their complete lack of moral sense, or the crime that followed, none of it could be guessed at, even less understood. It had all taken place within themselves, as though each one only acted for the other. Anyone else there would have been an intruder. A stranger in the middle of this strange game that had no purpose but the exploration of evil, and which nothing could interrupt.

Whoever came near them at such times would be simply destroyed. There were no moral limits to the excesses they indulged in. They would plunge down to the very depths of horror itself until their untrammelled senses were sated. The taste of blood and of human flesh that scented their mouths pursued them like a terrifying roar.

Still hunched over his work, Dr Dennery coughed.

Henriette and Louise froze to the spot. Playing the dangerous game right to its limits, they didn't move. There they were in each other's arms, clear as day, picked out by the light flooding from the window, terrifying in their soiled nakedness, hardly daring to breathe in this incredible moment. There only remained one more thing to seal the blasphemy, to render completely infernal the sight that they were offering: their opened mouths pressed against each other, their moist tongues touched...

Above them, the shutter of their bedroom window clattered.

They both leapt back into the shadows. At the same time the doctor raised his head, glanced distractedly out of the window, turned off his work lamp and left the study, heading for his bedroom. The girls looked at each other, their eyes dazzled by their own brazen behaviour, their bodies stained with their crime, mouths filled with the wonderful taste of each other. For them, time had ceased to move.

"After that I could die," said Henriette, intoxicated.

"You know what we promised ourselves, one day."

"Yes. No one must find us. Our bodies must never be discovered."

"No-one will ever see Louise and Henriette dead."

"Look at us now, while we're alive!" Henriette cried to the assembled company.

Nothing around them spoke or moved.

"Too bad for them," Louise concluded. "They don't know what they're missing!"

And she took Henriette by the hand. Together the two of

them, like crimson ghosts, entered the house in silence.

The doctor had installed a little bath next to the bedroom so that his blind girls would not have to grope around in the corridor. They turned on the taps, hoping that the noise would not reach the ground floor, and watched as the bath filled up. Soon a pleasant, hot steam rose up. They stepped into the refreshing water and stretched out facing each other, blissfully happy and calm.

Little by little the water took on a red tint. They lay perfectly still, their eyes half-closed, legs entwined, weightless in this strange bath of blood, a perfect end to their wild night. Their calm faces were a picture of the most complete innocence. And perhaps they really were innocent after all. Henriette pulled the plug and the water flowed away. Standing in the bath they stayed to watch until the very last drop of purple liquid had gone. They grabbed huge white towels and dried each other off. Then they went to bed.

CHAPTER THREE

"Clack clack clack clack..." It's Dr Dennery's orphans going by. Hand in hand, like good little girls, in white socks and patent leather shoes, they were on their way to the church of Notre Dame de Bon Secours, there to hear the mass, which sadly they were unable to see. The famous eye doctor did all he could to give them a proper religious education.

He guided their little hands towards the font, indicating with a light pressure on the arm that they should kneel, for they were in front of the altar.

It gave the parishioners great pleasure to see the deep reverence of the two little blind orphans. A heavenly innocence shone from their young fresh faces on which were written all the signs of the most exemplary piety.

Each of them had a pair of dark glasses to protect their eyes, neatly arranged in a breast pocket, placed for just that purpose on their immaculate white blouses. Each wore a beige jacket and a pleated skirt of the same colour. They were charming, and the old ladies murmured into each other's ears: "Just like the two little sisters of the baby Jesus."

They imagined them in white communion robes, palms together, kneeling on either side of the child Jesus, while the baby benefactor spread out his protecting hands on their lowered heads.

Dr Dennery cooked the Sunday roast himself. It was a day of celebration and each trip in and out of the dining room gave him an opportunity to pat the neatly groomed head of one or the other of his girls.

The wayward pair submitted themselves calmly to this game, swaying under his touch, almost purring with satisfaction, closing their useless eyes and puckering their lips in gourmet pleasure. Dennery saw no vice in them and, innocent himself, harboured no trace of sensual feelings for Louise and Henriette.

They were, after all, little more than children, even though their silhouettes, showing through their night-shirts when they passed by a light, revealed their budding figures.

In the afternoon they played a game of backgammon, feeling the counters with the tips of their fingers.

In that way they were able to decipher which side had the points that showed the score. This gave rise to joyful disputes that always ended in laughter.

The good doctor watched the innocent games of his two little girls with delight. Then, when evening came, he retired to his study on the ground floor to carry on his researches.

Just after 9 o'clock, Henriette and Louise were standing in front of their bedroom window on the first floor, enjoying the phenomenon which, as night fell, brought the return of their sight.

It was like a photographic paper plunged into developing fluid which little by little reveals the image. First of all vague outlines, then shapes, finally the colours.

In a few beguiling minutes, with a surge of emotion that made them speechless, the power of sight returned to the little orphan vampires. They looked at each other, each immersing herself in the other's image, which now existed without the need to touch, to only imagine that which their hands revealed.

Soon it was time for these two she-wolves to go out into the street and set off running, straight ahead, with all the speed of their slender legs. For blind girls never ran: even with hands outstretched, the fear of bumping into something was always too great. Only sighted people ran. So the two orphans ran through the night, as far as their lungs would take them, until they were completely exhausted. Then they sat down together on the pavement and breathed in deeply.

To their right was the river, and further on a bridge onto which they climbed. There, above the water, with the illuminated Eiffel Tower and the overhead metro for company, they laughed at the top of their voices, crying out their happiness. Some passers by turned their heads to look at these two laughing children, alone on the bridge just before midnight. Then they hurried on their way, like all those who fear things they can't understand.

The girls moved on, but all they found was a tramp lying by the embankment.

"Ugh!" said Henriette. "That's not for us."

"Let's look for another of those silly kids, all fresh and pink like that one yesterday."

"So that I can bite his legs!" Louise cried, laughing.

"And I can split open his guts," added Henriette, going one better.

"The side is the tenderest bit."

"You really like to eat."

"I suppose you only want to drink?"

"Well, you'll laugh, but I would much rather eat a piece of little girl or a little boy. Young men don't really attract me."

"Yes...biting off a piece of juicy, plump baby..."

"Screaming at the top of its high pitched voice..."

"But little children are all asleep at night."

"Maybe we'll get a chance one day!"

And so they went, skipping, clutching each other by the hand, like two ogresses from a fairy tale, lighting up the night with their crazy presence.

Thus passed the summer.

Each night brought the death of some unlucky stranger, young ones, fat ones, stupid ones.

It was like a game. Who, at that time of night, could fail to notice Louise naked in the middle of the street, or Henriette, crying hot tears, sitting by the road side like an abandoned child? When one was visible the other was always waiting in ambush, never far away. Dawn saw them return, laughing, their faces daubed with fresh blood. The good Dr Dennery knew nothing of these nocturnal escapades. And each morning the street resounded to the 'clack clack clack clack' of the white sticks of the two little orphan vampires out on their daily walk, clutching the arm of their kindly benefactor.

Thus passed the summer and came the winter. Bringing almost endless nights, lasting from 7 o'clock in the evening until 8 o'clock the next day.

Nights of more than twelve hours, full of blue light and, always, new adventures.

Paris belonged to them.

Now they knew how to get around the city using the metro or the bus. As soon as the evening meal was over and Dr Dennery had shut himself up in his study to work, they edged their way outside.

He never came upstairs to open their door and look at them asleep. Nor was he surprised to see them go to bed so early. What else could they do? Cinema, television, even reading, were out of the question.

When they returned, at around five o clock, he was sleeping soundly.

Then they would rest for a few hours and when they woke up they were blind once more.

Their big discovery was the huge cemetery of Père-Lachaise. It became their regular stamping ground. They would get there around 10 o'clock and wander through the paths until midnight, delighting in every moment's discovery of a new tomb, a monument or a statue.

Then the hunt would begin.

It was a curious thing that when their sight returned, the winter cold vanished. A sort of interior warmth enveloped them. But with the first glimmer of dawn the icy air fell on their shoulders and never left them.

One night, after a particularly long adventure, the sky was lightening and growing pale as they crossed the doctor's garden. Then they felt as though a cold hand was running along their bodies, seizing the back of their necks...while all the time their sight slowly ebbed away. It was on tip-toe and trembling that they opened the door, staggered upstairs, reached their room, took off their clothes, shivering, and slipped under the covers. They slept side by side, warming each other up, promising themselves that never again would they allow the daylight, that stole away their eyes, to take them by surprise like that.

One afternoon, their fascination with cemeteries led them to feign exhaustion and go up to their room at 4 o'clock, so as not to inconvenience Dr Dennery. He had to make a visit to the hospital and a friend wanted him to stay for dinner.

As he went to get his car out of the garage he wished good evening to the girls, who were on their way upstairs.

Soon a deep silence spread through the garden and over the house. The girls' plan was to reach the cemetery before it closed, to see it while it was still busy.

They slipped outside and turned left, towards the entrance of the nearest tube, the location of which they now knew well.

'Clack clack clack clack,' went their white sticks. It was just on half past four, the daylight was fading but it was still bright, and Henriette and Louise found themselves in that grey, indistinct fog which was their no man's land between blindness and sight.

In the corridors of the metro people moved aside to let them pass, while others offered them a seat; hands took their arms to guide them and helped them onto the train when it came in to the platform; then they were off.

The trip was fun, counting the stations as they passed. They got lost changing lines, then found their way again. And their hearts filled up with joy, because now the shapes of things were getting clearer in front of their eyes. The first colours were appearing, emerging from the blacks and whites. That meant that up above the sun was down, that the shining night was setting in.

At last they came back up to the surface. There in front of them, opposite the exit of the Père Lachaise metro, stretched the high wall of the cemetery. A little further on were the big open gates. Men, women, children were passing in and out. It was not yet five o'clock.

Drunk with a suppressed, hidden pleasure, Henriette and Louise held each other demurely by the hand as they entered their domain with dainty steps.

'Clack clack clack clack,' went the two white sticks. And how sad it was to see these little things walking along in their white dresses, with thick woollen socks to keep out the cold, their hair neatly tied in plaits, holding in front of them those painted sticks, symbols of their misfortune.

"So young, how is it possible?" murmured an old woman.

"It's such a shame," her friend agreed.

Henriette and Louise could hardly suppress their giggles, for now, in front of their dazzled eyes, as soft as a kiss in this blue tinted universe, was emerging the world of shapes and of colours. Their dark glasses were folded away in their breast pockets, so eager had they been to fill their eyes with the wonders of white marble and sculpted stone that made up their kingdom. At times they forgot to keep their eyes fixed on the distance, as they turned their gaze from one side to the other.

But who would have suspected that two fake blind girls would be walking in the cemetery at the end of an afternoon?

❝Don't drag behind, children, it's getting dark!"

With the tip of her boot, Madame Maude de Bésieux cleared some dead leaves from her husband's grave. General de Bésieux had died young in a tragic car accident ten years earlier. She was no longer in mourning, but when she visited the grave she still dressed in black and wore a little veil on her hat. The general, who had never had the chance to show his mettle in war, had yet given her these two children before he died. A girl and a boy, Clotilde and Jérôme; she was twelve-years-old and the boy just two years younger.

As for Maude, she was what people call "a fine looking woman". She had tried to do her best for the children. By a strange coincidence, Jérôme, who was already wearing glasses, had been examined by the best eye specialist in Paris, a certain doctor Dennery.

Maude was not particularly interested in the children. She made sure they had a good Catholic upbringing but it was all for show and without tenderness, without warmth, with no real intimacy between the mother and her offspring. Consequently they were somewhat deceitful and sly, very withdrawn, jealous of each other and quite ignorant of the facts of life.

Now the last rays of the sun were gilding the white crosses, their shadows lengthening across the graves.

The general's wife, having assured herself that the children were still following a little behind, pressed on unconcerned.

She saw the big path that led to the main gates.

She decided to wait there for the stragglers. It was good for them to be alone sometimes, without the constant presence of their mother.

So her thoughts strayed to other things. Realising that their mother was granting them some moments of freedom, Clotilde and Jérôme dragged their feet. Suddenly the boy grabbed his sister and pointed.

"Look! Two blind girls."

Two neat little girls were passing nearby, walking along, all sweet and timid. 'Clack clack clack,' went the iron tips of their white sticks among the dead leaves.

It was a rarely visited spot.

"Shall we push them over?"

"That would be wicked," said Clotilde, who, if she wasn't afraid of Hell, where a General's daughter could certainly never end up, at least feared purgatory.

"It's just for a laugh," Jérôme replied. "Do you reckon they've got white knickers like their dresses?"

Looking up girls' skirts out of the corner of his eye was his favourite trick. So far it was his only vice.

"No," Clotilde insisted. "That's very naughty. You shouldn't do that."

"Are you coming or not?"

"Mother's a long way off! She'll be waiting for us."

Without replying, Jérôme crept from tomb to tomb, following after the two little blind girls. Clotilde came close behind him: the reservations she had expressed earlier should be enough to save her from a few hours of purgatory, she decided.

The spiteful pair were now only a few steps from Henriette and Louise, separated from them by just a row of monuments. Jérôme was seized by a mad passion to see the little blind girls' panties, and perhaps even to touch them furtively before running off. His face hot and his teeth clenched tightly together, he imagined the feel of the material under his fingertips.

As far as Clotilde was concerned, since her brother was solely responsible for what was going on, she would be quite happy to see the two girls grazed on the gravel of the path, covered with bruises and cuts-or better still, with their knees bleeding. Laughing deep down inside, she imagined them uselessly waving their arms about in the air, looking for something to pull themselves up with, for obviously she and Jérôme would have to snatch away their white sticks.

Everything happened very quickly: Jérôme picked up a broken tree branch, jumped up onto a tombstone and stuck the branch between the legs of the two blind girls, who tumbled into one another with a double cry.

Louise was on top, Henriette below her, and only the latter's dress rose up enough to show to the enraptured eyes of the red-cheeked Jérôme a pair of knickers-not white, as he had

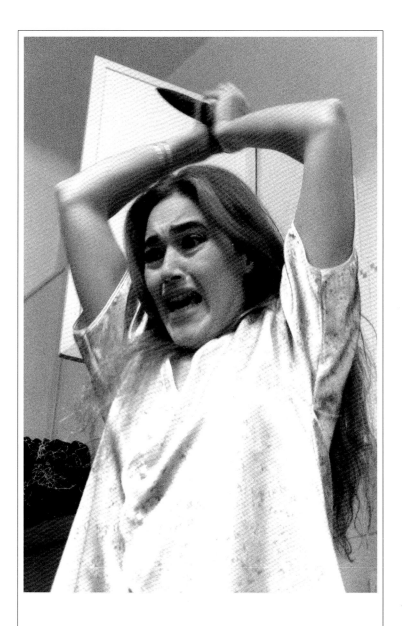

Cast:

Alexandra Pic — Louise, one of the orphan vampires
Isabelle Teboul — Henriette, the other orphan
Bernard Charnacé — Doctor Dennery
Natalie Perrey — Sister Martha
Anne Duguël — Mother Superior
Nathalie Karsenty — The Wolfgirl
Anissa Berkani-Rohmer — Nicole
Véronique Djaouti — The Batgirl
Nada — Virginie, the sick girl
Brigitte Lahaie — A girl
Tina Aumont — The ghoul

Original script: Jean Rollin from his book
Director of photography: Norbert Morfaing-Sintes
Sound: Francis Baldos
Assistant to the director and
director second crew: Jean Noël Delamarre
Director of production: Lionel Wallmann
Production Films ABC , Lincoln Publishing,
Francam Inter Service Corp.
The Batgirl costume: Sylvain Montagne
Editing: Natalie Perrey
DIRECTED BY JEAN ROLLIN

imagined, but green, a very bright and luminous green. He didn't dare to touch them, for already the girls were standing up, helping each other almost as though they could see. Pulling his sister after him he began to run, back up to the path again. Then they both sped off, away from the exit and the main gate where the general's wife was already waiting for them, peering into the darkening cemetery.

Those who cannot see, even if it is only during the day, develop certain senses. Henriette had *felt* Jérôme's eyes on her green knickers. She rubbed her thighs as though to remove the stain and turned to Louise, speaking softly: "They've climbed up behind the graves."

"I think there's two of them."

"Right. I'm just starting to see properly. There's almost no sun now. We're going to get them."

They picked up their sticks and began to run.

"We're lost," grumbled Jérôme, furious at having to admit it in front of his sister who was watching him sourly, arms crossed.

"*You're* lost."

"So do you know where we are?"

"I was following you. It's getting dark, mother will be furious. I don't see anyone we can ask."

"We have to go back down. We came uphill."

"And come across those two blind girls?"

"They won't still be there...Come on."

They strode along through the tombs and found themselves on the path where Henriette and Louise had been walking earlier. They began to descend. A few dozen yards in front of them some trees hid the exit. They carried on, with the row of graves to their left full of menacing shadows.

Jérôme was watching the tombs from out of the corner of his eye. Clotilde began to feel sorry that when they ran off they hadn't taken the blind girls' white sticks as trophies.

Suddenly Jérôme stopped, his mouth agape, staring wide eyed at what was in front of him. Clotilde turned her head to see what had caught her brother's attention, and put her hand over her mouth to stifle a cry of surprise.

Dimly lit, framed by the arched opening of a tomb, an extraordinary spectacle confronted them. A female form in a white dress, smiling and stretching out her arms towards them.

The shock rooted them to the spot. Their thoughts froze. Not for a second did they think of the two blind girls. Whatever was standing now before them could obviously see, beckoning with its arms, hands open, staring them straight between the eyes.

Clotilde held Jérôme back but there was a lump in the throat of the general's son. He watched enthralled, pulling away from his sister.

"Let's get out of here! Come on, it's a mad woman!" she cried.

Fascinated, he recovered some of his courage: "No, take another look. It's just a girl the same age as you!"

He was no longer afraid. He even took a couple of steps forward. Clotilde let go of him, refusing to move, but watching eagerly. Jérôme asked: "What are you doing there all by yourself?"

The apparition took a step backwards into the mausoleum: "Come...I want to show you something."

"Such as what?"

"Can't you guess?"

"Tell me. I want you to tell me."

"If you come in here with me I'll show you my bum."

Gasping for breath, beside himself, still he hesitated. He wanted to be quite sure of what had been promised: "No kidding?"

Without a word she twirled round, pulled her dress up and leaned forward, showing him her knickers. At this moment Jérôme should have recognised the green panties that he had seen when the two blind girls had tripped over. But he was beyond rational thought now. The dress fell back and the girl turned to face him again. Stepping backwards, she disappeared into the shadows. Nothing was visible but her two outstretched hands. Clotilde saw what was happening and tried to hold her brother back: "Don't go! It's a trap!"

But the boy rushed on into the mausoleum.

The blow from the white stick that he took just above the ear broke his glasses. He fell with a cry. Outside, Clotilde saw nothing, only that her brother had vanished into the shadows.

Silence ensued.

"Jérôme...Jérôme, what are you doing?"

Silence.

Clotilde was torn between her desire to run and her curiosity: what if Jérôme and this girl were up to something? And why be afraid? Jérôme had already said that the little temptress was only the same age as her. Why be scared of a kid? She thought about the two blind girls. Same white dresses, apparently the same age...Impossible. The girl that Jérôme had gone off with could see. And she was alone. That decided Clotilde, who marched right up to the entrance.

"Jérôme...Jérôme, are you there? Answer me!"

A muffled and barely recognisable voice reached her: "Come and see! She's naked in my arms!"

That was really too much and Clotilde marched straight in. She took the second white stick right in the face. It broke her nose. She just had time to see Jérôme in the distance, lying face down, with Henriette sitting on top of him. Then the laughter of the two orphans rang out, and Louise, following her friend's example, threw herself onto the body of this second victim.

A few moments later Madame de Bésieux, along with two caretakers, set off in search of her children.

She never found them, and she would spend the rest of her life haunting the offices of the lost person's bureau, unable to come to terms with what had happened. All day long she would sit by the telephone, waiting for a call from the run-aways. It wasn't so much their leaving that upset her as their disloyalty. Children of the General, indeed!

While Maude de Bésieux was wandering through Père Lachaise with the two caretakers, calling out for Jérôme and Clotilde in a voice now furious, now pleading, some astonishing events were taking place in that sacrilegious tomb.

Henriette and Louise had stripped the general's children completely naked so as to have a good look at them. They were not, like their victims, simply cruel and perverse. What inspired them was a healthy curiosity about the human body, a genuine desire to understand the purpose of the sexual parts.

So they saw, they touched and they knew.

Then, as Jérôme and Clotilde began to moan, showing that they were about to come to, the little orphan vampires ate them alive.

Each of them had their very own victim. Their hunger was limitless: the bodies were fresh and fleshy, chubby, plump, and naked. Henriette took hold of the sister's two tender, juicy buttocks and pigged herself on them, while Louise smeared herself with the blood that spurted from the brother's split jugular. Then they ripped out the guts, plunging their hungry young faces into them and gorging themselves on the blood and the flesh.

When the children were dead, the girls set about hiding the dismembered, bleeding bodies. They found a stone in the floor with an iron ring attached to it. Beneath would be the coffins and the family vault. Together they prised up the stone. There was a gaping hole below it. They threw the bodies in, taking care not to look down, because they didn't like dead things, being themselves so full of life and joy. Then they lowered the stone down again. All this time they had been naked, like their victims, so as not to cover their beautiful white dresses with blood. Now they straightened their hair, dressed themselves and set off nimbly down the long path.

'Clack clack clack clack,' went their two white sticks. The orphans smiled to themselves, because they could see quite clearly in this blackest of nights. They found it difficult not to laugh when they saw in the distance the silhouettes of the General's wife and the caretakers. They heard her calling: "Jérôme! Clotilde! Answer me! It's mama here."

Henriette and Louise were now walking along a very old path, through graves that had been badly neglected and had fallen to ruin. Louise stopped: "Listen. I can hear a rustling sound."

She pointed to a monument just like the one they had been in: a gothic chapel, with an iron grill and a sort of altar inside it. On top of the altar stood a broken vase holding the remains of a bunch of wilting flowers. On the ground, covering the stone that marked the entrance to the vault, were some iron wreaths decorated with artificial blooms, the whole thing desolate with age, with rust, with spider's webs. The rustling sound was coming from above the altar, just behind the cracked vase. Intrigued, the girls went to have a look. Lifting up the vase, they found a little animal stirring about in the dead leaves. Roughly the size of a hand, it was a bat with a flat head and big ears, the sort that people call vampires because they are carnivorous. They don't generally grow to more than four or five inches in this part of the world. The cold winters usually killed them.

Henriette picked it up softly, taking care not to damage its membranous wings. The animal stopped moving, feeling the warmth given off by the human hand.

Louise looked at it, fascinated.

She stroked its throat delicately with the tips of her fingers, and the veins in its neck began to throb. Henriette sensed that her friend was offering herself unconsciously to the vampire's kiss. In a hesitant voice, her mind and body in a turmoil, Henriette asked: "You want...you want its teeth? Do you want it to bite you?"

Unable to speak, so strong was her desire, Louise nodded.

Cradling the bat in her hands, Henriette brought it up to Louise's throat, like an offering, in a gesture full of tenderness.

The animal sensed the living flesh and, concealed behind its spread wings, it put out its teeth and quenched its thirst slowly at the source. Louise closed her eyes in ecstasy as she felt the blood flowing through two tiny holes. She sighed, breathed deeply, and for the first time in her life knew pleasure.

Henriette, trembling with emotion, lifted the bat away and laid it down on the dead leaves behind the vase.

Two red points were piercing Louise's white throat.

The blood was still flowing out of them. Without thinking, Henriette seized her friend by the back of her head and brought her own mouth close. Louise, eyes still closed, did not resist. Henriette put her teeth there, where the bat had drunk, and sucked. Her friend's blood flowed down her throat, intoxicating her. It was not an act of aggression, as it had been with their victims, but an act of love between them, a true communion. In that moment, and also for the first time, Henriette, too, knew pleasure.

"**Driiing!**"

Ali, the late night grocer, looked up to see who had come into his shop.

Tears of pity welled up in his eyes when he saw two pretty little blind girls, not much more than children, with the white sticks that they waved cautiously about in front of them.

"And what would you like, my little misses?"

"Sir, we would like some alcohol."

There was a silence. Ali looked closely at them, certain that they couldn't see him. They were minors. Alcohol? But how could he doubt such innocent handicapped girls?

"And what type of alcohol?"

"It doesn't matter. It's a present. Strong alcohol."

One of them held out her hand in which there were some ten-franc pieces. Not much. Ali had a look, counted them, then thought for a second.

"Gin, would that do?"

"Yes, sir, of course. Is it nice?"

Ali had never drunk alcohol, but the little blind girls wouldn't know that.

He decided to avoid the issue: "So it seems. For people who like that sort of thing..."

He took the coins from Henriette's hand and closed her fingers around a bottle of gin. The girls nodded politely and inched their way towards the door, chorusing in unison: "Thank you, sir."

Thoughtfully, Ali watched the little martyrs walk away.

As soon as they were by themselves again, in a lonely back street, the two girls leaned against a wall while Henriette opened the bottle. They had to cauterise the little holes in Louise's neck. It didn't take long. Henriette soaked her handkerchief in gin, washed the tiny pin pricks and it was done. They didn't say anything, but each took a drink, one after the other. Then they decided to walk back home. It was early, and the bottle was still full.

Midnight had long come and gone when, on tip toe, they

pushed open the garden gate. Several passers-by had been astonished to see these two young blind girls in white dresses sharing a bottle of gin, pouring it straight down their throats. And the strange sound of their sticks, 'clack clack clack clack,' an irregular noise matching the rhythm of their unsteady gait, added a bizarre dimension to the scene. But the passers-by hurried on their way, convinced that they were imagining things.

By an unfortunate coincidence, just as the girls were making their way across the garden, Dr Dennery's car appeared. The good doctor was returning from his dinner. He got out, opened the door that the two girls had only just managed to close before jumping behind a bush, drove his car in, got out to close the gate again and was just about to get back in the car to drive it into the garage, when a shining object, rolling into the light of his head lamps, caught his eye.

It was an almost empty bottle of gin which, having rolled, turned over and spilled out its contents.

Dennery picked it up and stared at it in astonishment. Then he looked around him. To his left were some thick bushes, a tree, then the wall. The branches seemed to be moving. Someone was hiding there, behind the tree, between the bushes and the wall. The doctor was afraid for his two little girls. He leaned into the car, opened the glove compartment, and took out a little pistol that he always carried with him. He pointed the gun at the bushes and said in a firm voice: "Come out of there whoever you are!"

There was only silence, but this silence was alive. He knew now that there really was someone there. He fired.

He heard the sound of someone running along the wall.

Straight away Dennery got back into his car, turning the lights full on to flush out the thief or drunkard he had taken a pot shot at. But he only succeeded in lighting up the wall. The night was too dark to see the intruder. In any case, the noise had stopped now. Still, the doctor wasn't quite satisfied. He ran to fetch a powerful electric torch from the house and scoured the garden. He didn't find anything. Whoever it was must have climbed back over the wall.

Dennery put the car away in the garage and hurried upstairs

to make sure that nothing awful had happened to the two girls. He pushed open the door of their bedroom, saw that they were sleeping soundly, and went into his own room, after having bolted the front door. The rest of the house was well protected by shutters and iron bars across the windows. As soon as the doctor had gone back downstairs, Henriette and Louise got out of bed, trembling with fear...Henriette had been wounded in the arm.

It was only a graze, but it was bleeding. Their terror, when they realised that Dennery had spotted them, then seeing him shoot, had completely dissipated the effects of the alcohol. Henriette in particular was shaking all over, her teeth chattering, remembering how the bullet had cut into her skin.

They had to staunch the bleeding.

Louise knew how to stop Henriette losing too much blood. She fixed her mouth to the wound and left it there.

A pleasant feeling of torpor crept over them both. Soon they were asleep.

When they woke up the next morning, blind once more, the lips of one were still fixed to the arm of the other.

It took all their willpower to separate themselves, to stagger into their clothes and down to the dining room where Dr Dennery was waiting for them.

They would never again mention the events of that night.

'Clack clack clack clack,' went the two white sticks on the echoing stones.

Amplified by the silence inside the church, the impact of the iron tips rang out and bounced from wall to wall.

Two worshippers, kneeling among the empty chairs, raised their heads, disturbed from their pointless prayers.

Seeing the young blind girls who had just come in, they quickly added them to their benedictions.

In this late afternoon, Henriette and Louise were still sightless. Spring was coming and the days were stretching out, as though they were fighting back, refusing to give way to the healing night. The two girls had again taken advantage of the doctor's absence. He was away at a banquet and was not due back until the following day. The event was taking place in Le Havre and he would be spending the night in an hotel. His two protégés were now familiar enough with the house for him to feel quite safe leaving them alone, but with plenty of food and some money, "just in case..."

He had hardly gone when they too were off, tapping their white sticks against the pavement, heading for the entrance to the metro. They ducked inside and took the line for the Gare de l'Est, getting lost, laughing and falling about, to the great surprise of the other passengers. They had decided to be in a crowded place when their sight came back, then they would leave Paris and go hunting in the wild. They had been missing the little country graveyards and the old days of the Glycines orphanage. Now they had the whole evening and night before them, to travel, gorge themselves on whatever took their fancy, and return before the doctor got back.

Then some words overheard by chance had led them to this old church, with its columns and arches, its niches with statues, and corner cupboards for candles and prayer books. They went inside.

Neither of them were believers, so the presence of all the religious symbols, the holy water and the altar, didn't worry them at all. They didn't feel the slightest discomfort or nausea, which, if you believe the old stories and legends, should have been expected from two little orphan vampires. On the contrary, the atmosphere inside churches attracted them. The quality of the sound, the coolness, the awkward presence of the two or three silent worshippers. For Henriette and Louise, who had never before actually seen a church, this was going to be a voyage of discovery.

As evening fell, vague outlines of things became visible, still edged by darkness. Everything was blurred, in black and white, not really identifiable, and so it took on for them the mysterious allure of a ghost ship sailing out of the fog. But what really fascinated them was the pulpit, towering over the rows of chairs, all of them empty. Except for two.

Henriette and Louise sensed in minutest detail the presence of these two unknown creatures: their breathing, a light scraping of a shoe against the floor — a wooden floor, more sonorous than the stones — a sudden movement. They walked down the central aisle, between the rows of seats, straight towards the altar. Their sticks brushed lightly against the chairs, marking the way for them. 'Tick tack tick tack,' went the iron tips on the wooden legs and bars. Finally they stopped, without a word. They didn't really know where they were any more. The darkness inside the church was delaying the return of their sight. All they were aware of was the blue light that surrounded them and some dark shapes, like the huge wooden pulpit with its curving staircase.

They hesitated. They could sense the eyes of the two people watching them. Then one of them, a woman, stood up and headed towards them. Louise was the nearest. The woman seized her by the arm, forcing her down and muttered, loudly enough for Henriette to hear as well:

"You are before the altar....You must kneel."

All they could make out was a vague silhouette, which frightened them. They obeyed and both of them put a knee to the floor. The woman, towered above them, looking down with a sort of evil joy, as though she took pleasure in seeing these two children bend to her command. There was a noise to their left. Instinctively they turned their faces towards it.

A man who had been praying had risen to his feet and was heading quickly for the door, his steps echoing. Louise tried to call out, to make him come back. Fear, inexplicable, hideous fear, was gripping them for the first time in ages. But no sound came from her mouth. The noise of the door closing told them that they were now alone with the woman.

Their sharpened senses picked up some strange vibrations. This person they couldn't see was wicked and cruel. Perhaps even worse than they were.

The evil that emanated from her paralysed them, they were unable to tear themselves away. Then the woman, standing now between the two kneeling orphans, made it worse. She squeezed Louise's arm even harder, seized Henriette, and forced her also to the ground.

"Kneel! With both knees!"

The poor girls put their second knee onto the floor. The act had been transformed into one of humiliating submission.

They tried to pull away, but the woman's firm grip held them prisoner. Then, taking advantage of their uncoordinated movements, with one kick she knocked away their white sticks, which rolled right up to the foot of the altar.

Henriette and Louise were disarmed. They raised their heads to look at the woman who had them in her power. All that they could see, in a sort of grey fog, was a chin, and a mouth with thin, tight lips. The rest of the face was hidden under a domed black felt hat, the brim pulled down. A plain and simple cloak covered her body. The woman shook them, hissing: "I sense evil in you...The devil...You exude wickedness and death."

As far as the girls were concerned she was just a freak, typical of the creatures who haunt such places. One of those bitter women who seem to live only to judge and condemn others. Not for a second did they think they themselves could provoke such feelings, could generate so much hatred and anger. They didn't know that churches, temples, mosques and synagogues, as well as all the 'good people' who frequent them, are ill-starred places for little orphan vampires. But they did understand that the woman in black would be as pitiless as any fanatic.

The woman was beside herself, enraged by their very existence and bent on their destruction. Terrified, made even weaker by their loss of confidence, they began to writhe about spasmodically, pulling at the fingers that held them still to their knees. A thrust forward sent them sprawling towards the altar. They grabbed their sticks, stood up and began to run through one of the aisles heading for the door. Kicking the chairs out of her way, the monster tried to cut off their flight. She was right at their heels when the girls reached the door and threw it open. The train station lay opposite. They ran on, hoping to lose themselves in the crowd. Night was falling, but it was still too bright for them to see properly. For the poor girls everything was a uniform grey, and the dominant blue, which was their light, made hardly any impression at all on the foggy mist that enveloped them.

They ran through the building, right up to the tracks.

Looking back, they saw the woman, easy to identify in her dark cloak and felt hat, but hazily outlined, the vague contours making her even more terrifying. She was after them. Programmed to destroy. An exterminating angel. Muffling a cry of terror, they ran on.

There was a train at the platform, just moving off. The woman was no more than a few steps away, and walking with the deliberateness of an automaton.

Louise grabbed hold of a carriage door, opened it, seized Henriette by the hand and pulled her in. They rushed along the corridor, banging their sticks about to clear people out of the way and let them through. Slowly, the train chugged along the platform.

Colliding against the compartment doors, stumbling through the connecting passage, they reached the next carriage just as the train left the station.

One after the other the suburbs sped past the window of the empty compartment. Henriette and Louise could see quite clearly now, but the colours had still not returned. It was no more than a matter of minutes, soon they would be the only ones able to see in the night. Panic stricken by their adventure, they spoke together in flat, toneless voices:

"She couldn't have caught us."

"Where's this train going?"

"Away from the station and that church."

"Are you sure that she didn't get on?"

"The train was already moving, she wasn't as young as us, she can get stuffed!"

"We ought to kill her, bleed her dry, chew her up so that she can't bother us any more!"

"I'm going to look in the corridor, I'm not happy."

Henriette stood up, pulled the door open and stuck out her head. There was a silence. From behind, Louise saw her stiffen. Then Henriette turned round and looked back at her friend.

She mumbled, beginning to shake as though she were suddenly cold. "She's out there...Looking through the carriages..."

Terrified, Louise stood up. They grasped their white sticks and shrank back to the far end of the compartment, against the glass, as far away as possible. The train sped northwards...

The face of the woman was suddenly framed in the glass of the corridor window and her stare pierced through the two girls.

At that same instant, just as night fell over the countryside, their sight returned. The colours flooded back in, awash with the customary dominant blue, and as always this sudden light dazzled them. They closed their eyes for a second, and when they opened them again they were staring right into the face of the woman who had pursued them all the way from Paris, had climbed aboard the moving train, and now had them cornered in this empty compartment.

It was the face of death itself.

A pinched face with sunken features, the lips no more than a thin line. Her eyes burned with a fever, of hate, of barely contained madness. With a big, sweeping gesture, she slid back the door and took a step forward, cutting off their escape.

Now she was in the compartment, overjoyed to have these two terrified girls at her mercy, their outstretched sticks trembling in their hands.

In a hoarse, deep voice she spoke to them: "I will make you crawl before me, foul creatures, you have soiled the holy place. To think that I was praying for you..." She gave a terrible and joyless laugh. "For you! But who should have pity for two evil creatures of darkness?"

The mad woman advanced towards them once more. Henriette and Louise raised their arms, but with the same sad and sinister laugh the crazy creature snatched away their sticks, just as she had done in the church. They tried to protect themselves with their raised arms.

Her eyes starting from their sockets, each one of her hands grasping a white stick, the woman struck out. She struck again and again, first of all at their protecting arms, to force them down, then at their heads, then their faces.

The train pulled into a small station. They had left the suburbs and were already in the country. Voices sounded out in the corridor, but the crazed woman, in the grip of her hatred, heard nothing: she went on hitting the two girls as they slid slowly towards the ground, almost unconscious.

The voices stopped: a group of five young men were getting on, staring in disbelief at the incredible sight: a woman beating to death two little blind girls in white dresses, their faces swollen, their eyes full of tears, unable to protect themselves from this virago.

The young men looked at each other, then flung themselves onto the woman, snatching the sticks away from her, grabbing her around the waist to hold her back. The woman struggled as though possessed, cursed, and struck out one last time at the little blind girls with her heavily shod feet. As Louise and Henriette lay twitching with fear, the five boys, without a word, dragged the woman out into the corridor.

No one ever knew how the door came to be open, but just the same the woman was hurled through it. She disappeared into the night with a strangled cry, just as the train lurched forward at top speed. The boys shut the door again and all of them understood one thing: that was the last they would ever hear of that old woman.

They went back to the compartment.

Just a moment earlier Henriette had been looking out of the window and had seen the woman fly by, her arms flapping, screaming as she was flung off into the night. It had all been over in seconds, but this vision of hell would remain forever engraved on her mind. She fainted and collapsed against Louise who held her close, choking with pain and terror.

It was impossible not to be moved by such a sad sight. Two of the bluff northerners were unable hold back their tears. The other three set about comforting the young girls with gentle words, then settled them comfortably on the bench.

They dried their tears. They kissed them softly. From out of their pockets came combs to tidy their hair.

They did such a good job that soon the poor pale cheeks became as red as little apples, and only a short while later the girls were laughing out loud, full of gaiety and joy. They could see the five boys perfectly, but without anyone suspecting it in the slightest. And they could read on their faces the sympathy, the pity and the tenderness that they had aroused.

Henriette and Louise left the train at the next stop. There was a touching farewell. The boys went with them as far as the platform and, when the train set off, their five faces were glued to the window to look one last time at the two girls, both walking very carefully, with dainty steps, towards the exit. 'Clack clack clack clack,' went their two white sticks.

'Thock thock thock thock,' went their sticks on the muddy ground of the country road, quite deserted at this time of night. It was after 8 o'clock, and lights shone from the dining room windows of all the farms and houses. They were on the outskirts of a village, the road led away from the town square, away from the high street, the station and the main road. It was a track that ran through the fields, parallel to a B road that led to another identical village.

Henriette and Louise knew, for they had asked someone, that the last train for Paris left at exactly 12:28. They would be on it. And before dawn they would be properly tucked up in bed in their room in the 16th. When Dr Dennery's car returned in the morning, when he opened the door - carefully so as not to wake them - they would be smiling smugly in their beds, full of the blood that now they were hoping to drain from some stray yokel. This would be their revenge, for at the moment when their pointed teeth were planted in his flesh, when the hot, thick blood was coating their throats in a long, soothing stream, they would recall, laughing inside, the menacing harpy whom their friends had hurled from the train, sending her crashing onto the tracks. While they were walking they saw again in their minds the boys' faces, their tender smiles, their big, muscular, country boys' bodies. Henriette wondered what it would be like to know love in those arms. She should have offered herself to them in the compartment. But...that would have meant giving themselves away, betraying themselves...Louise also imagined being in the arms of one of the boys, he was crushing her to him, climbing on top of her. Would it be as good as the coming midnight feast, as delicious as the blood that would soon fill her mouth and throat?

The road they were on led straight to the cemetery, of course. Very soon they were there. They looked it over, ready to go in. It was just like the one near the orphanage, the one that they had so often haunted.

They pushed the gate open.

In the blue light they felt the soft warmth that only came at night, when their sight returned. They had come home, and in order to enjoy the feeling they took off all their clothes, every stitch; now they were completely naked.

The moon was their sun. Without saying a word to each other they stretched out, side by side, on a mossy, cracked tombstone; it was a very ancient stone, not like the cold marble used today. The light of the moon made their white bodies gleam. Their sticks were leant against the stone cross that towered over the tomb.

Both of them were still, as though they were no longer alive, but their bellies rose, their chests heaved: they were breathing. Like that, naked on the grey stone, so young, so delicate, so slender, so childlike, the little orphan vampires were perhaps even more touching than before, when they had been two poor blind girls beaten by a madwoman. If those boys had seen them like this, offered up to the wind, stretched out so still, hand in hand, they would have carried them off and never let them go, as if they were two cute little dolls made out of moss.

The gate squeaked. Someone was coming into the cemetery. Footsteps were crunching the gravel of the path as two people approached. What to do? They were surrounded by statues: marble angels, a mourner, a couple of Christs. Henriette and Louise sat up, pressing their hands together in an attitude of prayer, heads lowered. In the darkness it was hard to see them clearly, they could easily be mistaken for two statues, the whiteness of their bodies would add to the illusion. They could only hope that the intruders, too busy with what they had come to do, would not notice the white sticks leaning against the stone cross. The girls stayed perfectly still, watching as the silhouettes approached.

It was two kids, come to meet here after nightfall, away from prying eyes. They took no notice of the watching statues and sat down on a nearby tombstone. The boy took the girl awkwardly in his arms and they kissed, nervously caressing and touching each other. Not far away the two strange flowers of the cemetery watched, feeling the hunger rise within them. Still as stone, Henriette and Louise were enthralled by what they saw. The boy's hand moved along his girlfriend's thigh, pushing back the skirt, exposing the plump flesh. His other hand was under her jumper, kneading a heavy breast.

Certain now of their invincibility, the orphan vampires went into action. As the boy's hand left the girl's thigh to slip inside her panties, they began to move. The two lovers heard a noise, turned their heads and saw two naked ghosts floating towards them, lips drawn back from pointed fangs, ghosts with cruelly shining eyes.

Henriette grabbed the girl's hair with both hands, pulled her head back, and even before she could scream, had planted her teeth into the swollen and throbbing veins, feasting herself on the liquid that flooded into her throat. At the same time Louise threw herself onto the boy, biting him again and again, making a gaping wound. Then, as he lay dying, she bent over and drank her fill.

As her hand stroked the healthy young victim he was seized with convulsions. Without realising it, as she was conscious of nothing else when she feasted, her fingers had found his cock. It was still hard. Her hand closed around it, squeezing and rubbing it. Joyfully, she plunged her face into the bleeding hole in his flesh, covering herself with blood. As he died, the young farmer emptied himself in a final spasm into Louise's hand, which was still gripping his cock. It was like a signal, for at the same time the girl that Henriette was sucking dry also gave up the struggle.

The little vampires staggered to their feet, exhausted but happy. Henriette saw Louise's face smeared with red, and in a hoarse voice, begged: "Let me taste your blood...Now...Right now!"

"Come and drink it from my mouth, then."

Louise opened her arms, offering up her sticky lips to Henriette as she came closer, almost shyly, looking at her friend with a strange sensation, her eyes moist with tears. This was no act of bravado, as under the doctor's window. There was no danger here, no-one could look up and discover them. No sound could betray them or give them away. They were alone at night in this country graveyard, and one of them was offering up her red mouth to the other. As their lips touched their eyes also met, *seeing*, and caressing each other with their gaze.

This was not like the fierce passion that had drawn them together in the garden. It was with an infinite humility, with a tenderness that came from the timid and precarious depths of her very soul, that Henriette brushed her lips softly against Louise's damp mouth. It was hardly noticeable but now, sealing her lips, Henriette had a purple speck like a teardrop of blood. Their eyes stayed fixed on each others' and, right there and then, their passion for life and for each other was so strong that the dawn could have risen and neither of them would have made the slightest movement.

From now on, each one of them would carry into her daily night, as a sort of final vision, the face of the other, fading slowly, growing dim, pale and vaporous before it finally disappeared.

With an effort they turned their heads away, breaking the tie that bound them together.

Now once again they were the charming and cheerful criminals of a moment before. The flash of seriousness that had lifted them up briefly to the summit of a vertiginous elsewhere had passed. Once more they were the little orphan vampires, ready to rush headlong towards the sorry fate that, somewhere, was waiting for them.

One day there would be nothing, absolutely nothing, left of the little orphan vampires. And then, as Henriette had insisted, no one must ever find them.

Her eyes sparkling with malice, Henriette smiled at the bubble of fresh blood on Louise's mouth.

"You're like a ghoul whose just eaten!"

Louise laughed.

"Well, the other day, in the park, you ate some! Don't you remember?"

Henriette smiled, thinking of the young boy. Then it was time to go. Hand in hand, white sticks and clothes under their arms, they headed for the gate.

When they got there Louise, seeing the main road, pulled Henriette back.

"Come on...Let's have some more fun!"

Adrien Levalier glanced at the dashboard display. Nearly 10 o'clock. It would be a good two hours more before he reached Tierson. And tomorrow he had to be up early. He accelerated angrily. To hell with the speed limit.

At this hour there would be no one about in the little village.

He drove through without seeing a single living soul and pressed his foot to the accelerator when he reached the main road again. In the beam of his headlights he saw on his left a row of cypress trees and the wall of a little cemetery.

As he came up to it he seemed to see something white moving behind the gate.

Adrien Levalier was not the superstitious type. But what he

saw next gave him such a shock that his jaw dropped open and he began to scream without even knowing it: his headlights had flashed for a second across the gate where he had seemed to glimpse the white shape. In the yellow light he now clearly saw two naked ghosts, covered with blood, staring straight at him. They were clutching the bars of the gate, and the wind was rustling their long hair. But the most frightening thing of all was that the ghosts were laughing.

Adrien lost control of the car, spun the wheel sharply to the right, smashing into a tree. The left hand door, ripped away, flew across the road and crashed at the feet of the two ghostly orphans, who didn't flinch — nor did they stop laughing.

They saw that the head of the unfortunate Adrien Levalier was now hanging at a painful angle to the rest of his body. All danger passed, they pushed open the gate and ran towards the tree and the wreck that was wrapped around it.

"Look out!" Henriette shouted. "It might catch fire and explode!"

"You watch too many films!" Louise sneered.

They approached the body. A trickle of blood was running from its head down to the ground where the earth swallowed it. Louise dipped her finger in and when it was all red, she licked it.

"It's better when they're still alive," she said.

"Of course," said Henriette who had long since realised: it's drinking life that is good. Death is much harder to swallow.

They walked away in disgust. But there was no point in tempting fate and so they set off in search of some water to wash themselves with. They found no stream or river, nothing. Finally they arrived back at the village.

"We can't put our clothes on over this blood."

"It's not even dry. We have to..."

"Look!"

In the middle of the empty village square there was a fountain with a trough. A spring flowed up through it. Without stopping to think they ran over and clambered up into the trough. They began to soak themselves, playing and splashing about in the water. The bell in the little church, two streets away, rang out 11 o'clock. A hairy head looked out of a lit up window, and a man shouted at the shining silhouettes that he glimpsed in the basin: "Clear off, you little devils!"

Laughing, Henriette and Louise ran through the streets, dripping, carrying with them their white sticks and clothes.

They dressed again under a porch and set off.

'Clack clack clack clack,' went their two white sticks along the station road...

"The year is 1488. Before us, for us, they are preparing the four day festivals to celebrate the inauguration of the Grand Temple of Mexico. The successor to Montezuma 1st, the emperor Ahuitzotl himself, stands at the summit of the pyramid, readying the first sacrifice. The priests surround him. For many moons the population has been in a state of ecstasy. All the town is decorated, everywhere there is singing, dancing and rejoicing. Contrary to the Aztec calendar, certain signs indicate that the return of Quetzalcoatl, which should have taken place in 1467, may well come to pass during the events that are now being prepared. Down below I see the long, endless procession of the victims. There are rumours that there are more than one hundred thousand of them. These four days will stand as the biggest voluntary suicide in all the history of the world... In fact it is a ritual communion: blood and flesh. Blood that will flow without ceasing, sacrificial flesh that the faithful will devour at the foot of the pyramid. There is talk of at least twenty thousand victims on this very first day.

I am pressed against Louise, my side touches hers, our fingers are entwined and our bodies quiver with impatience. Already, under the clamouring of the crowd, the procession of those who will have the honour of being killed by the emperor begin to climb the steps that lead to the temple. From where we stand it looks like a column of ants. Their faces are raised up, some of them are smiling, for soon their blood will be feeding the gods. The pyramid is huge, more than a thousand steps high. The one marching at the head is already a third of the distance. I see Ahuitzotl at the summit, plumed, holding in his hand the obsidian dagger.

At his side five priests, similarly armed, follow his lead; everything must be finished by the night of the fourth day: the slaves disembowelled, their blood spread on the steps of the temple, their hearts devoured by the high born, their flesh eaten by the people.

When the thousand steps are completely red, then Quetzalcoatl can return. My throat is dry with desire and with tense expectation: the first victim is now up on high. The priests seize him, lay him on the stone, the emperor strikes, opening his chest, plunges his hands into the cavity, seizes the heart and, so that all may see it, holds it - still pulsing - aloft above his head that is adorned with the feathers of multi-coloured birds. A dreadful cry rises from the crowd.

The emperor carries the streaming trophy to his mouth, bites, rends it in two, shreds it. At this sight the people hurl their frenzied cries into the heavens. Already another man is stretched out on the stone. The knife is raised once more, then brought down. This time it is the priests who pull out the heart while the servants roll the body away, immediately replacing it with another. The hearts are thrown down below where the high born and the nobles seize and devour them. The women snatch up a few morsels which, later that night, will be roasted or boiled for the cannibal feast. We now begin to see the thin red streams smearing the topmost steps of the temple. This evening, at sundown, every step will be stained. Every one. More than a thousand. And, at the end of the final day, the stairway will be nothing but a carpet of blood flowing from top to bottom, a moving carpet, with a smell at once sickening and thrilling.

Louise trembles and presses herself against me. For my part, I can no longer control my muscles or my nerves, and we embrace each other, we fuse together like a strange statue of flesh. What is happening before us is so unexpected, so incredible, that in spite of the daylight, our blind eyes see. Our vampiric weakness is put aside for this great blood-feast. Our real selves emerge. I know that I am Quetzalcoatl, the plumed serpent, and Louise knows that she is Murcielago, the bat goddess. Like her, I saw the first sacrifice, at break of day, and we were there with our eyes wide open as the people scrambled for the spoils. They flung themselves onto the heartless, broken-limbed bodies thrown down to them from the heights of the temple; each one went away with a leg, an arm, a torso, even a head in the hideous grin of death. Our eyes saw the pack of high born courtesans jump into the air to catch the still beating hearts that were tossed down to them; before our very eyes the slow file of thousands of victims climbed, climbed ever onwards: there were more than a thousand steps to climb. Men, women, children even, captives or chosen victims, all were naked and their feet became stained with the blood in which they walked. From above flowed the blood, down below grew the pile of living human bodies, an endless sacrifice. It is for us that this massacre is performed, to enrich our life, to give us breath; for us, so that we may appear in our resplendent godhead.

How can we not rejoice in this incredible slaughter, how can we not accompany this superb blood letting with the most rending of orgasms? How can we not respond with our bodies to the homage that is being offered us?

Our bellies flow with pleasure as the stones flow with bubbling blood. We greet the sun which, for the first time, rises without blinding us, without destroying our world. Today it is a scarlet sun, itself gorged on the contents of slaughtered bodies."

"All day long the festivities continued. At twilight, exhausted, we leaned against each other. Henriette, like me, is worn out. Our eyes have not stopped seeing, and the images that they show us continue as the red sun lights up the bath of blood. And now that night falls, our day begins, stronger than before, more alive, more scintillating. The priests, and the emperor whom they surround and protect, have now left. Gone are the nobles, gone the crowd. All now go to pray to us and to feast on the morsels snatched from panting bodies, prepared for the ritual feast. The area around the pyramid is deserted, the glistening steps give off a smell of suffering and of crime, the mutilated bodies are piled up on all sides.

We wander, living goddesses, breathing the fragrances that intoxicate our senses.

No rest for Quetzalcoatl, no rest for Murcielago: in a few hours our worshippers will return and the victims will be let loose from the enclosure. Again will be formed the long procession on the steps to the altar. Again the obsidian knives of the priests will be raised. How many dead this first day? It's still not enough. The river of blood must not run dry.

The stones soak it up but are still stained. The thousand steps leading to the temple are red. Soon they will shine, when fresh sap covers them like a living sea in perpetual motion.

Our naked feet feel the shape of the stones, but between this stone and our skin crunches a curious substance that flakes off, shattering into little pieces, turning into dust, splitting up into a multitude of particles: dried blood.

No one knew in the sleeping city that this very night, thirsting, drinking with their eyes, two goddesses, serpent and bat, Quetzacotl and Murcielago have returned to haunt the Grand Temple of Teotihuacan. Only the torn remnants of the massacre, the piles of broken bodies that rise here and there about the pyramid, are witness to our solitary wanderings. And beneath the moon, which is our sun, standing on the five hundredth step of the huge stairway, mid-way between the summit and base, we stretch our arms, our hands, towards the town as though to cover it with our loving protection.

We stand now before the sacrificial stone, right up high. It also is red, with the same red that covers the stairway. Below a lake is formed, so deep, so full, that it can never run dry. I want to plunge my hands in it, cover my face with it, smear my body with it...

Henriette and I throw our useless white sticks into this dreamlike vista which gives us the power to see both day and night. The two sticks bounce, jump, tumble from step to step, and at last disappear over the edge, where they bury themselves in the massed heap of bodies."

"With the day comes again the murmuring of the crowd on their way to the pyramid.

At the same time the long sacrificial line reforms.

The emperor and the priests are already at the top: they have ascended the thousand steps at the first light of dawn, so that the people may not see them strained during their long and tiring climb.

Louise and I are hidden as on the previous day. And, as on that day, the red sun does not blind us. Our thoughts register all that our eyes show us: the images unfold in three dimensions and in living colour.

Everything begins again the same as the day before. An endless stream of blood flows from step to step as the bodies are thrown to the eager, outstretched hands. And tomorrow will be the same as today. The number of the dead surpasses that of the living, the collective madness calls, crying out to the goddesses to return, to show themselves in human form.

Finally it is the last day, and we stand at the foot of the pyramid.

Total stillness reigns. Even the wounded cease to moan, the people fall silent, the high born, the nobles, right up to the priests — all watch us without a word, for we are the returning gods, the resurrection of the plumed serpent and of the bat.

Naked, hand in hand, heads held high, we begin our climb. A thousand steps to reach the sacrificial stone where waits the first victim of this final day.

For until nightfall it is we, the gods, who will kill.

The venomous fangs of the serpent, the razor sharp teeth of the bat will pierce the concealed hearts that must be torn out to be brandished before the eyes of the crowd.

Thin, pale silhouettes, we climb, and our feet tread firmly in the fresh blood that once more covers all of the thousand steps, rising over our ankles, smearing our calves. The sweetness of this liquid, the dull smell it exudes, fills our heads, and intoxicates us. The very worst excesses come to our minds, tempting us. One shared glance and we stop, a third of the way up.

Everyone is watching us, alone there on the stones. Above us the emperor, the priests, are nothing but tiny unmoving statues. Down below, the crowd seems blurred, indistinct, frozen in expectation. We are alone and our solitude grants us the freedom for any indulgence. We kneel down then, arms outstretched, bodies arched, we stretch out, we lie down on our backs, facing towards the top of the pyramid. Then the ceaselessly flowing blood covers us, paints us from head to foot, filling our waiting mouths, clotting and sticking to our hair, flowing over our backs, our buttocks, our thighs, covering us with a frightening warmth.

The sight must be horrifying, for a growing murmur rises from the admiring and appalled crowd: the resurrected goddesses accept the blood offering, they cover themselves with it, they gorge themselves on it. And when we stand up again, dripping, reeling from the overwhelming smell, caressing our wet, glistening bodies with our open hands, the applause of the crowd rings out. We resume our climb upwards, like two scarlet beasts, and all the time our hands touch our shining, glistening bodies, reeking of the blood that clings to us, pressing our breasts, squeezing our thighs, digging in our nails, making our own blood flow so that it mixes with that of the sacrifices.

We climb onwards, side by side, like two skinned animals, and our all-seeing eyes are fixed on the sacrificial stone. There waits the first victim of this fourth and final day of the festival. As soon as they saw our human forms, as soon as they recognised our sex, the priests chose for us the strongest male. His muscles ripple across his naked body, for he pulls on their arms, presses against their thighs, trying to tear himself away from the stone on which the four men are holding him. Is it the fear of finding himself naked before these two young girls, themselves also naked and dripping with the blood of his companions? Is it the fear of revealing his desire to be disembowelled and to have his heart devoured by these god-children? His mouth is open as though to cry, but no sound can emerge. His head bent forward, he sees us and the barbaric sight that climbs towards him is one from another world, that of the gods. Unable to control itself, his sex rises, his exposed member tenses like his other muscles, pleading with us to take hold of it.

"Clack clack clack clack," go our white sticks on the stones. "Splosh splosh splosh splosh," go our feet, squelching in the blood that splatters all over us.

We are almost at the summit, just a few endless minutes and we will be on the terrace, in the sacrificial space of the Grand Temple of Mexico, capital of the Aztec kingdom. It is the end of the 15th century, some thirty years before Hernan Cortes enters Yucatan."

"Standing in front of the flat stone, we look down at the fettered athlete as he strains his muscles, trying to break away. But he is held down by the firm hands of the slaves. The priests look at us in ecstasy. We feel their eyes on us, hungry for us. Our coming, in which even they did not believe, has driven them mad. They stand back, a few steps behind us, not daring to move. Only the emperor is at our side.

It is he who will dig with the obsidian blade into the powerful corpse of the prone man, open the chest, smash the rib cage, so that we may see the heart. We must take and taste it before it stops beating. We are not ghouls that eat the dead, like hyenas or birds of prey, but vampires who consume only the living.

The man tenses, seeing the arm of the emperor raised. A hoarse cry comes from his throat at the moment when the knife rips open his chest. A sound like the breaking of dried wood shows that ribs and bone are rending under the violence of the blow. The emperor reaches into the wound, parts the flesh, and we see the heart. Quickly, it must be done quickly while the sacrifice is still alive! Our heads bend forward, Louise buries her face in the hole, her mouth wide open. In the excitement of the moment my own face pushes her's aside to take its place and plunge into this rent corpse as it writhes in the final throws of agony. Our serpent's teeth, our bat's teeth, our Aztec goddesses' fangs bite deep into the heart. The blood flows in waves down our throats. We are nothing but beasts gorging ourselves.

As we straighten up, both ripping out the heart in one swift movement, our eyes meet. I see madness and bestiality in Louise's eyes, and I know that she sees the same consuming passions in mine. The emperor recoils before the terrifying spectacle. The priests turn their faces, horrified by the incarnation before them of their very cruellest religious images; down below, the crowd, the high-born as well as the common people, let out a deep moan of terror.

In front of them all, Quetzalcoatl and Murcielago, in the

human form of two god-children crimson from head to foot, devour the torn-out heart. Staring into each other's eyes, the little goddesses give off a sickening sound with their hellish chewing. As the heart which separates their two faces is eaten away, the space between them is also reduced. And when at last the whole organ has been consumed, their purple mouths join in a chaste and innocent kiss, full of tenderness. And lovingly, almost timidly, the right hand of Louise, the left hand of Henriette, move away from the body, grope for an instant in space, then close together on the rigid member of the man lying on the stone, who has come to give his life for them.

At that instant, as if he had waited only for their touch, he dies. As he does so, in the same way that hanged men do, he fills the hands of the two orphans with his white essence."

It was daylight.

Henriette and Louise opened their eyes, emerging from their shared dream. The Aztec pyramid had faded away, they were in their beds at Dr Dennery's house.

The two blind girls got sadly out of bed, picked up their white sticks and, untangling their feet from the bottoms of their overlong night-shirts, they groped their way towards the bathroom.

They washed in silence. They didn't dare say a word: both of them were remembering their delicious dream. They hung on tightly to the last scraps of it, the final images, the lingering sensations. But, inevitably, the dream faded, vanishing at last.

When it was nothing more than a vague and very distant memory, Henriette said: "We ought to do something to make all that come true."

They looked at each other with their unseeing eyes and they both understood.

Downstairs Dr Dennery was pouring hot chocolate into cups.

He was waiting for his two little angels. The warm family atmosphere that this kindly man tried to create for the poor girls was for him a sort of paradise regained.

He called out: "Louise! Henriette!"

And, fondly, he heard the "clack clack clack" of two white sticks coming down the stairs.

"Ding dong ding dong," went the bells of Notre-Dame d'Auteuil on this Sunday morning. Dr Dennery and his two adopted daughters, Henriette and Louise, were coming out of mass. The two Dennery girls took their benefactor's arm. Both girls were dressed all in white, right down to the tips of their long thin fingers which were covered in old fashioned cotton gloves. Everyone looked fondly at these two sweet little children, by whose side the famous eye doctor walked so proudly.

He had long since given up trying to discover the cause of their illness. There seemed to be no trace of lesion, no microbe invasion, no virus, nothing. He would never cure them, he knew that now. So he had undergone a procedure for adoption, which had been quickly completed. He was now officially the father of Louise and Henriette. Thanks to this munificent gesture he enjoyed a considerable respect and deep admiration in the district. He was quoted as an example. People pointed him out to their children. There was even a suggestion that he ought to be decorated, so that if anything happened to him the children could be looked after by the Legion d'honneur.

Born of unknown parents, foundlings, they had now found a home....And yet they were becoming increasingly bored and frustrated.

Their whole life was arranged for them, organised by their father, with a time for study, a time for play — slim pickings for two blind girls — a time for them to go out for fresh air, and finally a time for sleep.

When at last they went up to their room on the first floor, which coincided more or less with the return of their sight, they always felt an enormous sense of relief. The doctor had cut down on his work. Near to retirement, he no longer taught any courses or went to conferences. His consultations at the hospital had now become home visits for a few specially selected clients. In other words, he was around the place almost all the time. Louise and Henriette had to be careful. Always alert, they had to watch everything they said for fear of giving themselves away. Their nocturnal adventures became more and more rare. For, since he was no longer working, Dr Dennery read and wrote late into the night. Not being so tired he was up until all hours. The fear of being found out was constant for the girls.

Would they have to settle down, only bite the occasional tender, juicy throat, conform to the pattern of their new life, taking on the role of Dr Dennery's good little girls? Or would they set themselves free, tear themselves away from their cosy little nest and take off for the heights of the Aztec pyramid; seek out the dizzy plateau where human flesh is eaten alive and feel the thrill of bitter blood flowing in their throats? An impossible dilemma? Absolutely not. They had already made up their minds.

They had to escape from their benefactor, regain their former freedoms. The Glycines orphanage now seemed to them a haven of security. With mother superior and sister Martha, so easy to fool, and that idiot Dr Hogineau. They missed their old room 136, the squealing of the other orphans at playtime and on their way down to eat.

"We could run him through with the spears from the living room wall."

"He's strong. What if he survives?"

"We could sharpen the points..."

"It would be better to suffocate him with a pillow when he's asleep. I saw that recently in a film."

"We're not strong enough. We need something quick and foolproof."

"I've got it! Let's just bite him, both of us, and suck his blood until he's dead."

"And he's going to let us do that?"

"We can sabotage his car."

"Push him in the Seine."

"What if we just run away and never come back?"

"Without killing him?"

"What difference does it make?"

"It's not so much fun. And anyway he'd come looking for us."

It was late and they were in bed. Feeling restless, they got up and began to pace about the room.

Somewhere in the house, a clock rang twice.

"Come on, let's go and have a drink."

"But...he might find us."

"He'll be asleep now. We might think of a plan."

They tip-toed down the stairs in their night shirts and crept into the kitchen. All was quiet on the ground floor, no light was coming from under the doctor's door. Henriette opened a cupboard where she knew there was a bottle of white wine used for making sauces.

They poured it down their throats.

"It's not as good as blood."

"But it's cooler."

"And it goes right to your head."

"Give it here."

They drank some more. Henriette wiped her mouth on the back of her hand.

"We have to think of something. Come on, let's have a look in the library, there are plenty of old books there with drawings of murders. That'll give us some ideas!"

They left the kitchen as silently as they had come in and went to the small, windowless room that the doctor used as a library. There, on a shelf, were some popular novels from the turn of the century. They had belonged to Dr Dennery's father. Henriette leaned forward, pulled some of them out by the spine, and suddenly a shiver ran through her. She took out one of the books and held it up to have a look. Louise rested her chin on Henriette's shoulder, and both of them stared in delight at the gaily coloured cover.

It was the 13th volume of Fantômas by Pierre Souvestre and Marcel Allain, called *The Uniform of Crime* .

The two fake blind girls stared wide eyed at the fascinating picture. They didn't hear the door opening softly behind them.

The illustration on the cover showed a waiting room with benches along the walls. At the far end was a glass door with the inscription 'Employment Agency'. In the middle of the room a pretty young maid was making a gesture of horror. The floor, the walls, the ceiling were covered in blood as though after a massacre...The servant girl's right foot was in the centre of a huge pool that was spreading out all over the floor...There was something about this picture that fascinated the little orphan vampires.

When the door was slammed suddenly shut they both jumped in the air, turned and dropped the book.

There, right in front of the horrified pair, was Dr Dennery, arms folded, a stern expression on his face.

He could see quite plainly that the two blind girls were looking at the picture on the book. He started to put two and two together.

Louise and Henriette stared dumb-stuck at the doctor, terrified by his sudden appearance in the library. For his part, a righteous anger was making his temples throb and swelling his chest.

There was a silence, then Dr Dennery said crisply: "I am glad to see that your sight has improved sufficiently for you to look at a book at three o'clock in the morning."

There was no point in carrying on the pretence.

Yet this man who had done so much for them was obviously so devoted to them that Henriette thought she might still be able to save the situation. She was the first to react. Louise was paralysed by fear.

Adopting her most angelic manner, Henriette said in a warm and tremulous voice: "Oh, papa, what a pity that you've found out our secret now! We were saving it for your birthday in three weeks time..."

Understanding what was going on, Louise joined in the game. "It's amazing what's happened to us. If only you knew how the dark started to fade away and we could see the shapes of things...How we began slowly to see, to recognise our surroundings..."

"To begin with we were so frightened...Frightened that it would go away, and that the darkness would come back forever..."

"But instead...Every day things have become clearer...Oh, it's not real sight yet, it's only a vague outline. We were so worried tonight that we came down to get a book and for the first time in our lives try and make out the words. Only the big ones. The ones on the cover..."

"And we did it! I could read! Papa, do you understand? And it was the same for both of us."

"Papa, it's such a joy, such a revelation...We wanted to be completely certain, you understand, before letting you know our happiness..."

"And so we set the date of your birthday as a test. If, on that day so dear to us, the miracle was still happening, we were going to read with our very own eyes a poem that we wrote especially for you in secret last Thursday."

The good doctor's heart leapt at the sound of these words. Without further ado, and unable to speak from the emotion that had brought a lump to his throat, he opened his arms wide. The two girls rushed to him and he held them close in a long embrace. His eyes shone with tears. He couldn't see the faces of Henriette and Louise which, squashed against their benefactor's chest, were having great difficulty in holding back their laughter.

There was no point in going back to bed. Dr Dennery began to question them closely, probing, trying to understand the why's and wherefores of the return of their sight.

They were in the kitchen. The doctor had made some hot chocolate and some cakes. A real feast. The clock rang out four. While they were at the table Henriette got up and, pretending not to be able to see properly, headed for the jam cupboard.

"What are you looking for, my dear? You only have to ask."

"Just a little orange marmalade, papa. And it's fun finding things for yourself, even if it is still through a thick fog..."

The doctor smiled, dunking a biscuit in his cup.

Behind him, with one swift movement, Henriette opened the door of the cupboard and pulled out the drawer where the knives were kept. Louise saw what she was doing, understood at once, and drew Dr Dennery's attention.

"Papa, when you looked at our eyes last week, did you notice anything different?"

"Your eyes were the same as always..."

Henriette raised her hands high above him, holding a sharp, pointed carving knife that was as long as her forearm.

Unable to bear the tension, Louise blurted out: "Do it!"

Henriette struck with all her force and the knife sank between the doctor's shoulder blades as he leapt up from his chair. He stood there, wavering, the knife jutting out of his back. Henriette ran to clutch Louise and the two girls watched as their victim flapped his arms about, staggered back to his chair, and finally fell with it onto the tiled floor. A silence ensued.

At last Henriette spoke: "Quick. Pack a few things and let's get out of here."

They rushed from the kitchen. They didn't see a hand grasp the edge of the table, then a second hand. Under their pressure the table shook, the bowls of hot chocolate rattled. It was Dr Dennery trying to pull himself up. The blade had not touched any vital organs.

Now he understood everything and, drunk with vengeance, he only hoped that he had enough strength left to destroy this spawn of hell that he had so naively taken to his bosom. Soon he was out of the kitchen, reaching the foot of the stairs as the two killers appeared at the top, their possessions held in their arms. He had cut off all possibility of flight: this staircase was the only way down from the first floor and out of the house.

Henriette and Louise were petrified by the sight of him.

The doctor stared up at them.

There were less than forty steps between them...

The two girls turned on their heels and raced to the other end of the corridor, passing their bedroom door without stopping. Dennery began to climb, certain that he had them cornered. The corridor was a dead end.

Henriette and Louise looked around for a way out. All that they saw, high above them, was the trapdoor that led to the roof. They jumped up onto a conveniently placed piece of furniture and, helping each other, disappeared through the trap as Dr Dennery set foot in the corridor. He just had time to see the tails of their night-shirts disappearing after them.

A silence heavy with menace settled over Dr Dennery's house. Lodged on the roof, pressed tightly against each other, the two girls stared out into the night. The blue light that was their day showed only an empty garden. No sound came from inside the house. What plan was the doctor hatching for their destruction?

In a low voice, Louise asked: "Do you think he's waiting for us down there?"

"With that thing stuck in his back he wouldn't dare climb up after us. Anyway, he's bound to be scared of us now."

"So what are we going to do?"

"Let's have a look."

Pressed flat against the sloping roof, they crawled to the trapdoor. It had a glass panel that they could look through. Henriette and Louise pressed their faces against it, and what they saw made them feel a lot better. Dr Dennery was indeed in the corridor, under the trap, but he had fallen to his knees. Unable to get up he had only a few moments more to live. His arms were raised, stretched towards the hole through which the girls had escaped. It was as though he wanted to seize them and strangle them before he died. His fingers jerked in spasmodic movements, as though he were actually holding the slim necks of the little vampires. His eyes were already glazing over. Laughing gaily, the little witches opened the trap again and lowered themselves delicately down onto the carpet, right in front of the poor doctor. He was still alive and, seeing them, he tried to speak. All that came out was a gurgling sound.

They had to finish him off.

Still laughing, Henriette and Louise seized him by the wrists and dragged him the length of the corridor, right to the top of the stairs. Then, with no more ado, they threw him down. Losing his balance, he tumbled, rolling head over heels all the way to the ground floor where he lay stretched out, motionless. In the fall the knife had been forced deeper into his back and now only the handle was visible. Louise and Henriette skipped down the stairs and rolled him onto his back with their feet. He was dead.

Henriette leaned over and peered intently at this man who had been their adoptive father.

"It's funny, she said, "I don't feel anything at all."

"It's not in our nature to feel love for do-gooders, nice people. Our passions are poisonous, our charms deadly. The conventional world they live in has nothing to do with us," Louise said.

"But there," Henriette said, pointing to her chest. "Don't you feel anything there?"

"Yes," Louise said. "For you! Just for you!"

"Well, at least we've known that," concluded Henriette with a touch of sadness.

Her friend rested her head on her shoulder, feeling again that sense of closeness they had experienced in the library when, unaware of the danger, they had been looking at the Fantômas cover.

"They'll never catch us," she murmured.

Together they looked down at the dead man, indifferent to everything he represented.

At that moment they were closer to one another than they had ever been.

A cat meowed outside the window. Henriette and Louise shivered.

"Quick, we've got to get out of here. In two hours it'll be daylight and we won't be able to see anymore!"

"Are we going back to Glycines?"

"It'll be easier for us there."

They picked up their white sticks, threw a few things into a bag and set fire to the house before they left.

"In a little while the flames will spread and everyone'll come to have a look! What if they find the body?"

"Don't worry. They'll never think it was us. Never. Two poor little blind girls! His adopted daughters, what's more. Why would we have done it? No, we're safe."

"But...running away...running away is like admitting it..."

"No. We were in shock. The thieves had beaten us up, we knew that they had killed our father, we just managed to escape. Being blind, we didn't know what to do..."

"So we went back to the orphanage. To get help from the mother superior and sister Martha."

"And that old fool Dr Hogineau!"

They both began to laugh as they ran towards the metro.

Fortunately the streets were deserted at the time, because two blind girls running is pretty unusual. But an unpleasant surprise was in store for them. The metro was shut. They would have to wait. Feeling just a little put out, they sat down on the steps, right next to the gate, leaning against each other. They were a sorry sight, one that would have drawn tears from even the hardest of hearts.

Their white sticks were resting against the iron grill. Anyone passing close by could have overheard them whispering happily to each other:

"If we're lucky we might inherit."

"There's not much left, now we've set fire to the dump."

"Don't forget the bank account, the shares, and then the land. Think how much a building plot in the middle of Paris is worth."

Far off they heard the sirens of the fire engines on their way to the doctor's house. Someone had raised the alarm.

"My eyes are starting to sting. It must be nearly daylight."

"Come on, let's hide. They'll be opening the gates soon."

Holding each other's hand they climbed back up the stairs and hid in the shelter of a doorway. Soon they heard the sound of the grill being slid back. The station lights came on and they rushed happily in.

They found the train they wanted still in the station, as it didn't leave until 8 o'clock. By the time they got on they couldn't see anymore. Some other passengers helped them find a compartment. They settled down opposite each other next to the corridor and, exhausted by the events of the night, they were soon dozing off.

Some time later that morning the ticket inspector shook them: the train was coming into their station. Still half asleep they took their bag, each one holding a handle and, a little unsteady, still not awake, they stumbled to the door, blinking, the full midday sun on their faces.

They smelled the familiar smell of the little town that they knew so well and they set off at once. They didn't even stop to eat. There would be plenty of time for that later: they were in a hurry to get back to the orphanage. They passed happily by the little cemetery and stopped at last in the shelter of a clump of trees. The big building was now only a few yards away. Already they seemed to hear the happy shouts of the orphans at play.

They smiled and went back to the cemetery. As easily as if they could see, they located a familiar tomb. They crept inside to wait for the night. Safely hidden, free of fear, with one's head on the other's shoulder, they went back to sleep and to their dreams.

It was the night of the full moon. Sister Martha was restless and couldn't sleep. She knew that the children were in bed, that the orphanage was peaceful. But, unable to relax, she was pacing up and down the corridors. If people asked about her nightly walks she would always say that she was "doing the rounds." But this particular night was different. A superstitious streak, which all religious people have, made her fear the first night of the full moon. Terrifying words filled her head, words like Walpurgis, werewolf, amok and possession, voodoo and witchcraft. So she walked the dim corridors, lit by a single light bulb in the stairwell. It was only there to stop anyone tripping over. A child going for a drink of water could break their leg, or worse, their neck.

The power was weak, a bare bulb of 60 watts burning all night just to show that there were stairs...But this white and sickly light threw enormous shadows, the banister, a cupboard, a plant on a stand, and who knew what else.

Sister Martha was a strong woman, her devotion to the orphans was proof enough of that. Still, she trembled and then shivered when she heard muffled footsteps down below, making the boards squeak as they headed towards her. She drew back against the wall, into the shadows, and waited. The footsteps stopped on the top stair and there was silence. A sliding noise told sister Martha that the mystery intruders were moving along the corridor towards the dormitories. She risked a peek: two shadows were plainly outlined against the wall. Two silhouettes that made her think of drawings, like the ones that had illustrated the fairy stories of her childhood, especially stories of gnomes and sprites: two tiny little people in stockinged feet, sliding silently along, holding their shoes in their hands, hunched forward, ready to run at a moment's notice.

Feeling more sure of herself, sister Martha took a few steps towards the silhouettes, to find out which of the girls were roaming the house in the middle of the night, and why. Then she stifled a cry of surprise. She had recognised, on the wall along which the shadows were slowly moving, the shape of two little sticks. "The white sticks!" she thought. "The two girls have come back!" Surprise and joy mingled in the mind of sister Martha. Surprise at the unexpected return of

Henriette and Louise, whom everyone had believed happily settled in Paris. And joy at the prospect of seeing again those two sweet children, whom mother superior always called her "little angels who see nothing but the good God himself".

As yet sister Martha could know nothing of the death of Dr Dennery, the burning of the house or the disappearance of his adopted daughters. Those events would only be reported later in the morning papers.

The nun hesitated. Should she call out to the two night walkers, interrogate them, or should she wait until the morning and then tell the mother superior?

Room 136 had been left empty. The two shadows slipped inside, closing the door behind them without a sound.

Everything fell silent once more. Sister Martha was alone in the sinister corridor.

The girl's return had brought in its wake a magical atmosphere, which now haunted the places where they had passed...And this mood was obvious, even to her.

So sister Martha didn't go back to bed. She sensed that something was about to happen, and that this very night a strange nocturnal life was taking over the orphanage.

Her rounds never went on beyond midnight. So, around half past twelve, the door of one of the bedrooms opened and out came two of the inmates, sure that the coast would now be clear.

Two girls in night shirts slipped into the corridor, one of them holding against her chest a tin biscuit box. They looked to left and to right, to make absolutely certain that sister Martha was not still about. Then they headed for the washrooms. Sister Martha, without letting herself be seen, followed them. They went inside and shut the door behind them. The nun trembled. What goings on would she discover? She decided to let the mother superior know about it and headed off as fast as she could. No sooner had she gone, when another door opened. It was Henriette and Louise. Their heightened senses had told them that two children were in the washrooms. So off they headed, their eyes shining, their teeth sharp: it was the night of the full moon and they too felt its effects.

Meanwhile, down on the ground floor, sister Martha was knocking at the mother superior's door.

In the washroom the two kids had opened their tin box. It

contained matches and a few cigarettes, plain Gauloises. With voluptuous pleasure each took one, lit up and began to draw. They fanned the smoke with their hands towards a little window that they had taken the precaution of leaving ajar. Just then the door opened.

The two girls jumped round, but were relieved to see that it was only the blind orphans. They recognised the two 'old girls' but didn't know that they had returned to the fold. Henriette and Louise smiled like wolves when they saw the appetising young things, their youthful bodies peeking through their thin night-shirts. They came in and silently closed the door.

Louise licked her dry lips with her tongue. Henriette moved towards the little brown haired girl who politely held the tin box out for her...

It was one o'clock in the morning and not everyone was asleep in the Glycines orphanage.

Mother superior went along the corridor ahead of sister Martha:

"The toilets opposite room 136, you said?"

"Yes...and in room 136..."

"It's empty."

"Not any more...They're back."

"Who's back? What are you talking about?"

"Your little angels...Louise and Henriette...The two blind girls."

"They are now living with Dr Dennery—his adopted daughters."

"I tell you they're here, mother, in their old room. They've just arrived."

"Good. We'll see about that later. First of all let's catch the ones hiding in the toilets. I suppose they're smoking...I hope it's only cigarettes. Where did they get them from? Does Dr Hogineau smoke?"

"Yes, I think so."

"They must have stolen them from his coat pocket."

While they were talking they had reached the door of the toilets. Mother superior put her ear against the wood, listening.

"I don't hear anything. You say there's two of them?"

"Yes. I recognised them: it was Genevieve and Odile."

"That doesn't surprise me! But we should be able to hear them yattering. Very well, let's see!"

Mother superior flung the door open dramatically and then, without making a sound, passed out cold. Sister Martha took a step forward to see what it was. She didn't faint, but instead threw up all her dinner, unfortunately right over the mother superior.

It was certainly a ghastly sight. Henriette and Louise were sitting on the tiled floor, cross legged, their faces smeared with blood. Henriette was trying to drink from Genevieve's opened throat, holding her stretched out across her knees. While Louise's teeth were planted deep in Odile's plump thighs, from which she was tearing a huge lump. A pool of blood was spreading across the floor in long streaks. Smeared over the walls and the fittings, it showed just how vicious the fight had been. The scene was exactly like the cover of volume 13 of Fantômas, *The Uniform of Crime*, the memory of which had perhaps served as an inspiration for the killers.

In a pile in the corner, in tatters, torn and stained, were the girls' night shirts that the little orphan vampires had pulled off so as to feel the naked flesh in their hands, under their nails and teeth, pressed against their own bodies.

Henriette and Louise looked up when they heard the door opening. Then the Mother superior had fainted, sister Martha had thrown up, and now a terrible silence reigned.

Henriette was the first to react. She leapt to her feet, seized Louise's arm and dragged her away. As the bodies of Odile and Genevieve rolled onto the tiled floor the girls leapt over the mother superior, who was moaning as she regained consciousness, bolted past an astonished sister Martha, and ran towards the staircase. They flew down it without stopping, crossed the darkened hall, pushed open the door and without drawing breath raced straight on into the night.

Mother superior quickly took the situation in hand. First of all she closed the washroom door and put sister Martha on guard outside. Then she went to her office and, with her eyes fixed on the crucifix hanging on the wall, picked up the telephone. She dragged Dr Hogineau from his sleep, convincing him in a very few words to come at once to the orphanage. Thirdly she called the police, got hold of the station chief, and asked for help. Finally she sat down on a chair and tried to work out a logical explanation for everything she had seen.

The alarm was given at 3 o'clock in the morning. While the orphans stayed locked in their rooms, the bodies were removed under the eyes of an appalled Dr Hogineau. Then the police began to scour the countryside. The villagers organised themselves into teams and they too set of in pursuit, armed with sticks, pitchforks and guns.

Right at the back of the barn, sitting in the straw in the very darkest, dirtiest and smelliest corner, the little orphan vampires were hiding.

CHAPTER THIRTEEN

They were trembling with cold and fear. Far off in the night they could hear the shouts as groups of villagers and farm workers called out to each other. But what terrified them most of all was the barking of the dogs. These, they knew, would be the most pitiless. If they were let loose, they would flush out the fugitives. And kill them. Inexorably, the new day was dawning. Already they could hear doors slamming in the farm buildings. People were starting work. They would be coming to feed the animals, there were sure to find the two girls. But fear and cold kept them from running any more.

Lights came on in the kitchen. At the same time two or three passing farm workers went in to drink some hot coffee and tell everyone what they knew. The story of the murder in the orphanage toilets had done the rounds. Passing first of all through the village, spreading from the institution and the little group around Dr Hogineau. Then from farm to farm as the search continued.

Henriette and Louise heard coarse laughter. They were making fun of them, talking about how they were going to stone them, hang them, throw them to the dogs. This seemed to cheer up the mob who, for the time being, were content just to blow onto their scalding hot coffee.

Henriette began to feel an overwhelming sense of tenderness for her friend. She realised that this was because they were doubtless both going to die before the night was over. She spoke in a calm and steady voice that didn't tremble, as though, now she knew the worst, all her fear had vanished.

"They mustn't find us here. We're surrounded, we can't run. They mustn't trap us."

"But they'll catch us outside in broad daylight...and it's coming soon...we'll be blind in an hour or so..."

"Let's try to reach the cemetery."

It was there they felt most at home. Louise was remembering the little bat from Père-Lachaise. A song was going through Henriette's head, but she couldn't remember the tune. At that moment someone pushed open the heavy door of the barn and came into the shadows. The fugitives held their breath. Then they saw a little girl carrying a pail and a three-legged stool. Her eyes were still blinking with sleep and she was yawning, having been woken too early by all the talking in the kitchen. It was the farmer's daughter, come to do the milking. She saw Henriette and Louise almost at once, put down her things and walked towards them, looking inquisitively at them. She was wearing a school uniform, her hair neatly combed, with two red ribbons holding her braids in place. No doubt it was her job to do the milking before setting off into the countryside to the little village school.

"Are you going to go on staring at us like that?" Henriette asked abruptly.

Oddly she didn't feel any desire to throw herself on the girl, drink her blood and eat her. On the contrary, she felt now for this stranger the same sort of feelings that she had just had for Louise.

"It's you they're looking for, huh?"

"Apparently," said Louise. "You can see that we're not like the others."

She had said that instinctively, not really understanding the sense of her own words. Deep down she guessed that their strangeness was obvious, that it was impossible not to see it.

"What are you going to do?"

The girl was not hostile or frightened. On the contrary she was staring quite openly at them, drawn at once into complicity with them.

"We're going to try to reach the cemetery."

Louise didn't even try to hide their plans.

"They say that you bite," the little girl said.

"Yes," Henriette said proudly. "We can if we want to."

The little girl stared at them, wide eyed.

"Is it because you bite that you're not like the others?"

"Something like that," Henriette agreed.

The girl came closer, intrigued. But she still remained safely outside the door.

"Will you bite me? If I come nearer?"

Louise and Henriette smiled.

"No, not you."

"Why? There's no reason not to..."

Her voice trembled just a little bit when she said that. She was afraid of being bitten. But at the same time she wanted to be. She didn't really think it could be dangerous. At least not fatal.

"Yes, there is a reason: you're our friend. You didn't shout out when you saw us. Because of that we'll never bite you."

A kind of trust had developed between them. It was warm in the stable, the sort of warmth that sleeping animals give off. The girl sat down on her milking stool, so as to be the same height as the orphans. They were leaning against the wall at the back, huddled together in each other's arms on the straw that covered the ground. Just a moment before they had been trembling with fear. Now they were chatting gaily. The two fugitive killers had become kids again.

"My name's Nicole," the girl said.

"We're Henriette and Louise," the orphans replied.

"Why have you got white sticks like blind people? Anyway, today they don't use them anymore, they have nice thin canes."

"We like these sticks. With these curved handles you can spin them round. Just like Charlie Chaplin."

"Are you really blind?"

"We can only see at night," said Henriette. "During the day we can't."

She said this as though it were perfectly natural. And Nicole accepted it without being surprised or astonished. That was just the way it was.

She came back to their present situation. "Why are they looking for you?"

"Because we've bitten some people," Louise said.

And she began to laugh, thinking about it. Henriette laughed too. Completely won over to their side, Nicole smiled at them.

"When you were very little were you still like that?"

"I don't really remember. I'm not sure," said Henriette thinking back. "No, it came later. At the same time as....when we were one or two years old. But before that, we were still not like the others."

"What do you mean 'not like the others'?"

"Well...different, you know?"

Louise interrupted:

"We've never, ever been like everyone else."

"So what are you?"

"We are us."

They collapsed into giggles, because they had both said the same thing at the same time. Nicole laughed with them. Henriette began to talk, and her eyes, her seeing eyes, took on a far off look when she described the childhood she had shared with Louise. A childhood still not so far away.

"When we were little we were already orphans. They found us in the snow, on the steps of a church. Perhaps we were sisters, perhaps not. In any case, we didn't care, no one ever knew that we could both see at night. In the day, I remember, we used to hear the other orphans talking amongst themselves of what they'd seen, films, pictures in books...So we waited until it was night. When everyone else was asleep we went down into the games room, you remember Louise? And then we looked at the pictures. And it was much better because then we discovered with our eyes what our ears had heard about."

She fell silent, dreaming. Then Louise took up the story. "Later we saved up to go to the pictures. We took money from people's pockets or we sneaked into the place. No one ever guessed that we had come from the orphanage. And later, when we found out about biting people..."

Henriette stopped her, she didn't want to frighten Nicole. "You see what a couple of fakes we are."

Once again, all three began to laugh. A cock crowed. The two runaways became serious again: the cock's crow heralded the approaching day, their approaching death. They were vaguely conscious of it, but wanted this moment, suspended out of time, no doubt their first real close moment with someone else, to last.

"But what do you bite with?"

Nicole understood perfectly that this was the big difference that gave the girls such pride. Louise drew back her lips:

"You see those teeth there, they stick out. At certain times."

"And...afterwards?"

"They go in again."

Nicole emitted an "ohhhhh" of admiration. Now she understood the terrible situation in which her two friends found themselves: sitting together on the filthy straw and the dung, their torn clothes stained and smeared, their faces dirty, their hair matted. Like convicts on the run!

She said: "You can't stay like that. I'll go and get some things for you."

She ran off. Louise and Henriette sat there, without saying a word, until she got back. Nicole was carrying in her arms some clothes that she laid on top of the stool. Then she went and filled her bucket with water from a tap in the yard, so that the girls could have a quick wash. When she came back into the barn Henriette and Louise had taken off their clothes and were naked, looking at the Sunday best dresses that Nicole had chosen for them.

"That's how we used to go to mass," Louise laughed.

"When we were little angels," Henriette sniggered.

"Jesus's two little sisters," Louise giggled.

Nicole put down the bucket of water and stared at the two girls. Seeing them in the barn naked and laughing like this made her feel strange. A cow mooed. It was an unreal atmosphere, a little bit of magic, particularly for the farmer's daughter. The simple nudity of these two girls, only a few years older than she was, had something holy about it.

Henriette and Louise, sensing Nicole's confusion, stopped laughing and turned to look at her, suddenly serious. For a moment all three of them stayed like that, looking thoughtfully at each other.

Nicole spoke, her voice a little uncertain: "Who are you?"

Silence. Then Henriette replied: "We are Aztec goddesses."

Once again there was silence. They all felt the power of this moment. Nicole said:

"You're not real goddesses?"

Louise said, almost to herself:

"All gods are real, because they're all imaginary."

Nicole was not entirely sure that she understood what Louise was trying to say. But a desire came to her, imperious, demanding. The desire that these two wonderful creatures, these marvellous Aztec goddesses, should touch her as she had seen in a painting in one of her schoolbooks that showed a god touching a human being. She asked the girls, whose white nakedness in this sad and soiled universe was dazzling her, if they would touch the tip of her index finger, as Michaelangelo's God had done for the first human being.

This time there was a long silence. It was only broken by a cock crowing in the distance; another one responded from nearby, the farm's own cock. It was another signal: they had to be quick. Time was catching up with them.

Nicole read their agreement in their eyes. She held out her right hand, drawing back all her fingers except the index which seemed to point at the little goddesses. Slowly Henriette and Louise lifted their arms and lightly touched this proffered finger. Nicole closed her eyes while life swirled around her, while the wild wind howled in her befuddled head, while the planet split into a thousand pieces.

When she opened her eyes again Henriette and Louise were still looking at her, smiling wickedly.

"Dress us like Aztec goddesses!" commanded Louise.

"Quickly! Before our magic vanishes with the dawn," said Henriette.

Feverishly, Nicole took the clothes and dressed the two girls. Soon they found themselves in little pleated skirts, white blouses and patent shoes. They laughed to see themselves rigged out like fairground dolls, all chaste and proper.

"We have to go," Henriette said. "The cock has crowed twice."

"After its last crow, it will be too late."

"Too late for what?" Nicole asked, still dazzled by the girls.

"To hope to live," Henriette said.

"But don't worry," Louise added. "We are immortal, after all."

"You know what you have to do? When we're gone you must go to the orphanage, on Saturday, say, when there's no school. It's right near here. Do you know it?"

"Of course. Everyone does."

"Right, well you must ask sister Martha to let you into the school room. On Saturday they let the little village girls come and play with the children. In the book cupboard you'll find a big album. It's called *100 Years of Magic Posters*. It's almost nothing but pictures of us. You'll see us as Indian maids with feathers in our hair. And also as red devils with shrunken heads in our hands. And as oriental dancers! Doing the dance of the seven veils! The Arab woman floating in the air; the Chinese girl crucified with knives in her body; the girls with crazy eyes, bursting out of their straitjackets; Houdini's mistress, with handcuffs on, diving into a glass tank full of water; Duga the magician, dressed only in pearls, making the flames of a brazier dance; the girl in a swim suit being sawn in two: all of them are us. The girl locked up with the tiger, the girl being sent to sleep to have her head cut off, to be cut into four, to be set on fire, to be stamped on by an elephant, it's us, it's us! All the little magic girls are Henriette and Louise!"

They laughed. Nicole listened to them wide eyed, her mouth agape, and in her head a crazy dance began, spurred on by the two goddesses.

"Well," Henriette said. "The game is over. We have to go back where we came from — to the cemetery."

"Are you going to die?" Nicole asked.

"Goddesses don't die, you'll see."

There was silence while the little girl digested this information. Then, pointing vaguely with her outstretched arm, she said:

"There's a road, down there, that goes that way. To the cemetery. It goes along by the river. You understand?"

They listened and then they heard the gentle sound of the endlessly flowing water.

"Show us."

They stood up and followed the little girl out of the door. For them it was still blue daylight, but somewhere in the farmyard the cock began to crow.

Henriette shivered: "Quick! Where is it?"

The little girl showed them the way. They had to cross the farm, run through the meadow, then at the far end of it was the river with the path alongside it. They hesitated: it was a long way. But for the others it would still be dark night, while for them it was the blue of day. Henriette took Louise's wrist.

Before going both of them looked back at their little friend: "Don't ever forget us, Nicole."

"But will I see you again?"

Henriette hesitated. It was Louise who answered: "Of course you'll see us again. Every time that you go into the barn like today, just before dawn, have a good look in all the corners. One day we'll be there."

Nicole watched them go, her hands in the front pocket of her school dress, because of the cold. When the girls reached the middle of the yard the kitchen door opened and three men came out. They spotted the runaways and shouted as they set off after them. In the meadow another group saw them and went to cut off their route. None of them were armed, but as they ran they picked up stones.

Henriette and Louise knew they were lost: three people were following close behind, four or five were coming from their left. They ran faster. A stone struck the back of Henriette's head and she felt the blood trickle down her neck, making her back sticky. Louise, a little way behind her, was hit on the arm, on the back and on the leg. Breathless, she cried out in pain. When she turned to look around a larger stone, more strongly thrown, hit her on the face. Her forehead was cut, the blood blinded her, she cried out again. Henriette pulled her along, giving her the strength to make the last few yards to the river.

They jumped straight in. The current seized them, dragging them under, lifting them up and then dragging them under once again, filling their mouths with a mixture of water and blood.

On the bank the group of farm workers decided not to venture into the river. They looked at each other shamefaced. None of them liked the idea of swimming in that rapid current at 4 o'clock in the morning. But since it was animals they were hunting, they would send animals in after them. They had three dogs on a leash. They set them loose. The dogs shot off like arrows along the river bank, snapping at the two little shapes that they saw moving away from them.

"If they don't drown first, the dogs'll get them," someone said. And slowly, rolling and smoking the first cigarettes of the day, they set off alongside the river, following the dogs.

Henriette gripped Louise by the hair with one hand while with the other she tried to grab hold of a root, a branch, a clump of grass, any solid part of the bank. Finally, she sank her fingers furiously into the damp earth and held on firmly.

The two bodies came to a halt. Louise was out cold and Henriette, facing the flow, gasping for breath, made desperate efforts to hold the unconscious body of her friend close to her, all the while keeping her own head above water. When she had regained her calm, she began to push and roll Louise up onto the bank. Then she pulled herself up and, covered in mud, haggard and out of breath, she collapsed onto the ground. Her hand still gripped Louise as if to stop her floating away again. A series of confused images flashed through her mind. She saw Louise drowned, her stomach full of water, washed up by a lock; she saw the peasants stoning a girl to death, that was Nicole; then she saw the little vampire bat in the cemetery being eaten by a cat; now she saw Dr Dennery getting to his feet with the knife sticking out of him, his hands stretched out to strangle her; but above all she saw the mad woman from the church with her soft felt hat, cornering her in the train...

Louise came to. She sat up, supporting herself on her elbows. She was very pale, her forehead and her cheeks were stained with blood, but the wound had stopped bleeding. Now just a thin trickle ran along her nose and dripped to the ground. Henriette, however, was suffering from the blow to her head. She touched it with her hand and it came away red. She stood up with an effort, held out her hands to Louise, and helped her to her feet. Both of them were shaky, their thoughts confused. Leaning against each other, they set off, climbing up the bank into open countryside. The main road lay ahead of them. And then the cemetery. There were only three or four hundred yards to go before they could hide out there.

They began to run. When they were half way there the dogs came bounding up from the old tow path that ran along the river. A few yards from the road they caught up with them, snapping at their legs. They fell, screaming, skin and muscle torn and bleeding. Locked fast together, girls and dogs rolled in a clump onto the main road. Henriette grabbed hold of the nearest two sets of snapping jaws, pushing the crazed beasts away with kicks of her feet. The third one bit Louise in the stomach. Henriette grabbed it by the skin of its back, lifted it off and hurled it against a milestone. Horrified, she saw Louise's torn stomach. Once again she pulled her up and together they tried to cross the road: the cemetery gate was just on the other side. The dogs growled, following close after them but not daring to attack.

Henriette felt dazed. Louise was moaning as she pushed her along, unable to carry her. At last they reached the gate. Henriette was on her knees for the last few yards, her fingers clasped around Louise's wrist. She let go to push the gate open with both her hands. At that moment, taking advantage of the situation, one of the dogs struck. He leapt onto Henriette's back and stuck his teeth into her neck. She screamed, grabbed the animal off her and threw it onto the road. Already her muscles were becoming hard, numb, a sort of paralysis was creeping over her: the back of her neck felt cold, she couldn't turn her head anymore. Now the gate was open. She dragged herself inside the cemetery, pulling Louise in by her feet. As soon as they were both on the other side she summoned all her strength and braced herself against the gate, shutting it at just the moment when the two dogs leapt towards her. One of them just managed to bite her on the arm, she felt the pain cut through her, right into her bones.

Far off the group of peasants were leaving the bank and coming towards the road, following the tracks. They would soon be there. With them came the day, and Henriette's sight was already fading, she could no longer see things around her with the same sharpness. She rolled Louise over onto her back.

Awkwardly, she cleaned her face with the palm of her hand, clearing off the mud, the grass, and the stones that were stuck to her skin.

"Come back...please...I can't make it alone!"

Louise opened her eyes, and smiled at Henriette.

"I don't feel very well...It bit me on the stomach..."

Henriette stood up, leaning against one of the graves.

Louise struggled to her knees, then, with her hands clutching her torn stomach, she also stood up, but still bent double.

Staggering, they moved away from the gate, heading deeper into the little cemetery.

The men were just then discovering the body of the dead dog by the milestone. They called out. The remaining animals answered them. Then they all moved on towards the cemetery.

At the far end, near the wall, were two big, hinged, iron plates. Beneath them was the communal grave.

The girls stopped in front of these iron plates, which were like a mouth closed over the bowels of the earth. Louise tapped her foot on one of them and listened to the vibrations. There was a long, deep echo. They didn't say a word, but both were thinking the same thing.

By this time the men had reached the gate. They weren't in a hurry: no one could hide out in this place for very long.

Far off a cock crowed. Another one answered it.

The men's progress was like that of the day itself: slow, inexorable, deadly.

Looking down at the iron plate, the girls heard their death approaching.

Louise felt her heart falter, spat out a clot of blood, and pressed her hands heavily against her stomach. She murmured: "My sight is getting foggy...it's fading...day is here."

Henriette felt her back grow stiffer as the paralysis spread. It was even difficult to speak now, every sound that she forced out caused her pain: "Quick...while we still can."

There was just enough time. The men had tied the animals up again, they were straining at their leashes. Taking a rest, the hunters lit up cigarettes.

Henriette and Louise raised the heavy cover. Henriette said: "Don't look down."

With her stiff neck she couldn't in any case. But Louise leaned forward and saw the black hole. For her it was already washed in the blue light that announced the end of their sight. Very far down she could make out the evil, miry magma.

Passing by the cemetery wall, Nicole pressed on into the open countryside. She had to cross the alfalfa fields to get to school. Her satchel was heavy on her back. She thought about the two runaways and knew that every time she went into the barn her eyes would be searching for them. Until the day when they were there again. As she walked she hummed a nursery rhyme:

My little rabbit
runs down the lane
he can't hear me now
and my cries are in vain..
Oh come back
little rabbit
to ease my pain....

Henriette could no longer see: the sun had come up over the wall and was lighting up the graves. She said, her voice a little shaky: "I think it's all over."

Louise wanted to answer, but blood was pouring from her mouth and her nostrils.

Standing in front of the grave they looked at each other with eyes that were already unseeing. Henriette spoke again: "Do you know why Aztec gods are different from all the others?"

Louise managed to whisper: "Tell me..."

"They are mortal."

And Henriette let herself drop into the pit.

Louise heard her fall. She gave out a great cry, and in her turn threw herself into the grave, letting go of the iron plate that slammed shut behind her.

A tragic silence set in.

Then things started up again, like a toy train set, stopped for a second by a sudden power cut, that begins again when the switch is thrown.

The men and their dogs searched all round the cemetery then, having found nothing, they left.

Nicole and her satchel were now just a speck, far off on the edge of the field of alfalfa.

The noise of the living faded away. Nothing now disturbed the silence of the graves. Except for a tiny bat, inside an abandoned tomb, flapping its membranous wings against a pile of dead leaves.

*(Translator's note: the story of the Little Orphan Vampires
is continued in Jean Rollin's next book **Anissa**.)*

The other books in the series are **Anissa, Les voyageuses** (The Wanderers), **Les pillardes** (The vagabonds), and **Les incendiares** (The Arsonists).